The
Bad Advice
of
Grandma Hasenfuss

Anne E.G. Nydam

With love for Marty Grundy,
a real-life Supergrandma,
(even if she can't crochet a bear trap).

The Bad Advice of Grandma Hasenfuss
An Epistolary Tale

From: dhasenfuss@something.com
Subject: **welcome back to technology!**
Date: Monday, October 12, 7:43 PM
To: melbahasenfuss@another.com

Hi Grandma,

I'm glad you got your e-mail fixed.

You didn't miss anything very exciting. School's not going so great right now. There's this kid who's giving me a hard time. Last week in PE I missed an easy kick in kickball and I felt like a total dork, and he started teasing me. And now every time he gets a chance he calls me a wimp, or makes fun of my name or something. There's a few other guys who hang around with him that are starting in on me, too.

But anyway, you probably don't want to hear about that stuff. Other than that I guess life is fine. I got 100% on my vocab quiz again on Friday. I went over to my friend Eric's house Saturday afternoon, but otherwise we had a boring weekend. Dad's going to bring home pizza for dinner tonight. Yum! I guess that's all the news here.

How's everything going for you?

- Danny

By the way, here's this week's new vocab list: abominable, calumnies, effectual, guffaw, predicament, rebuff

1

From: melbahasenfuss@another.com
Subject: **Re: welcome back to technology!**
Date: Monday, October 12, 9:51 PM
To: dhasenfuss@something.com

Dear Danny,

I, too, am glad to have the use of my computer again. It was quite exciting when the lightning struck, but you know very well I'm not one for too much excitement. All I want is a quiet life! I was just sitting at my computer looking up some crochet patterns, but there was a perfectly dreadful storm, with thunder and lightning zapping all over the place. Of course I counted the seconds between crash and flash, as I taught you, and I could tell the lightning was coming closer and closer. From my desk window I could see it striking up in the hills, and then on the other side of town, then just at the end of the street, then the tree on the other side of the parking lot.

Of course I should have shut down my computer, but I never think of that. Then there was a tremendously bright flash and simultaneously the bang like a cannon blast, and I jumped up as if I'd sat on a pin. The lightning came crackling through the wires into my computer and shot out through the cd drive like a white-hot electric snake. It came at me going for my throat, but luckily all my badminton practice came to my aid. Without hesitation I seized a large needlepoint cushion I'd made, and with one powerful and well-aimed swing I volleyed that lightning away from me!

Napoleon, who had been snoozing in the trombone, jumped up so high his back brushed the ceiling and his tail was bristled out bigger than an artificial Christmas tree. The lightning bounced around my study three times and knocked over my desk lamp, and then finally fizzled out on the floor. So luckily Napoleon and I were unhurt, but of course my computer was fried like an egg, and I had to

get a new bulb and shade for my desk lamp, too. Oh well
– these things happen, you know. Anyway, it's good to be
back in communication with you and your dad. I've
missed our daily e-mails.

Congratulations on the vocabulary quiz. Good
vocabulary is the key to success! At least, it can't hurt,
and if you can memorize all the spellings and definitions it
just goes to show you can memorize whatever else you
put your mind to, as well.

As for your objectionable classmate, of course I want
to hear about "all that stuff." You must tell me all the
details so I can help you figure out how to deal with the
problem. In the meantime, I hereby dutifully advise you to
tell a trusted adult at your school. The teacher will speak
with the boy, justice will triumph, and the problem will be
solved. Edgar Middle School will again become the Utopian
educational community it was meant to be. Voila!

Yours affectionately, Grandma

From: dhasenfuss@something.com
Subject: **jerks at school**
Date: Tuesday, October 13, 8:04 PM
To: melbahasenfuss@another.com

Hey Grandma,

You know I can't tell a teacher about John! Then everyone would call me a suck-up and tattle-tale as well as a wimp! A wimp and a nerd. That stupid vocab quiz just gave them something else to tease me about. I'm too bad at kickball and too good at spelling and stuff. Dad said I should just ignore them, but I bet Dad couldn't ignore someone whispering mean stuff in his ear every time he walks past. And don't tell me "sticks and stones will break my bones but words will never hurt me," either.

You said you wanted me to tell you all about it, so I'll list them.

There's John, first of all. He's tall, and wears all the coolest clothes, and sneers at everybody, even the people he calls his friends. He didn't used to bother me much, but last week in science he was dropping pieces of pencil lead and paper and stuff into the fish tank and I told him to stop, and he wouldn't, and I told Ms Diaz, and ever since then he's had it in for me. So you can see that I couldn't possibly tell a teacher about anything again or it will just be worse!

Then there's Rasheed. I'm stuck with him for my lab partner, and the whole time I was arguing with John about the fish he was clenching his fists and cracking his knuckles and looking like he would slug me if he thought he could get away with it. He scowls all the time and looks as mean as a Doberman dog.

Also, there's Austin, who's just a moron, and Marco, who's as big and tough as a high-schooler and cusses like — well, I'd be way too embarrassed to tell you the stuff he says, Grandma! That's a whole different sort of vocab talent! Then there's Connor, who looks like a sewer rat, and Brandon and Drew, who follow John around everywhere and agree with everything he says.

There's a few girls who hang around John all the time, too, mostly Hannah and Madison. They act like all they care about is clothes and shoes and they giggle at the stupidest things.

PE is tomorrow and I know I'm going to mess up again and it'll be even worse. Probably the whole class will start teasing me, and John and Marco and the others will think they're so cool. I don't know why they're the popular group anyway, but they are.

Anyway, I had no idea the lightning came right into your house! Dad only said your computer short circuited or something. I'm glad you're okay. If you're that good at badminton I bet you'd be good at kickball, too. Then when John says "My grandmother can kick better than you," I'll know mine really can. :P

        - Danny

From: melbahasenfuss@another.com
Subject: **Re: jerks at school**
Date: Tuesday, October 13, 10:17 PM
To: dhasenfuss@something.com

Dear Danny,

Yes, I rather suspected that you'd reject the idea of telling a teacher. And you feel sure that you're unable to ignore this John creature, either? You know those really are the two most sensible courses of action. However, if they cannot be done, they cannot be done, and we shall have to devise an alternate strategy.

As for sticks and stones, I quite agree with you. That is, I agree with you about the words. Brutal things, words. I once watched a verbal boxing match that left both combatants bruised and bloody. The first man, a professor of economics at our local college, accused the other, a politician fighting against a tax increase, of ignorance, and that was the bell for the first round. The politician led with an "I've had fifteen years of service to this community" to the jaw. But the professor shook it off and returned a sharp "studies indicate" followed, one-two, by a "9 out of 10 economists agree" that made the politician's eyes cross. The politician threw a "minor position at a minor institution," but it was a little wide. The professor dodged and parried with a "you insult our town's own highly respected college" that brought up an ugly welt on the politician's cheek. That's when the politican started fighting nasty. He aimed a "perhaps you can explain your failure to pay social security tax for your children's nanny" directly at the professor's solar plexus. I could see the breath go out of the professor, and he was utterly unable to put up any defense when the politician followed with a "people say you went to communist rallies when you were at college." The blood was pouring from the professor's nose by then, but he rallied and hit out with a well-aimed "why don't you tell everyone why your brother landed the contract for the high school renovation despite putting in the highest bid" that left the politician reeling. Pressing his advantage, the professor poured on the "corruption, arrogance, graft, and greed" and by the end of the drubbing the politician was out for the count with a black eye and a dislocated jaw. The crowd went wild. Each of us in the audience had a whole seat, but we only needed the edge...

But I digress. Let me just assure you that although your dad appears to have forgotten how upset he was when he was in sixth grade and Jeffrey Butchart called him "big-nosed frog-face," at the time he would certainly have agreed with your assessment of words. They can absolutely hurt, and you, my dear, need a respite from persecution. Perhaps it would be best if you simply lie low and attempt to avoid John's notice. I look forward to hearing how PE goes tomorrow, and whether it'll be as dreadful as you fear.

As for our name, just remember that even though ignorant people may make fun of it, (yes, Jeffrey Butchart teased your dad about it, too) Hasenfuss is actually an exceptionally lucky name.

Yours fondly, Grandma

P.S. I did notice and appreciate your circumspection in the matter of rude language. Should you ever need to report on such dialogue, you may respect my old-fashioned morals by using %$# and *@& and so on. I never say anything else myself, no matter how extreme the provocation.

From: dhasenfuss@something.com
Subject: **I hate PE!**
Date: Wednesday, October 14, 7:21 PM
To: melbahasenfuss@another.com

Hi Grandma,

PE was even worse than I thought! It was terrible! It was abominable! (See, I used a vocab word.) I tried to do what you suggested and lie low, but during kickball in PE I came up to bat, so everyone was watching me. I tried to kick just a mellow easy kick and maybe not give John anything to comment about, but it didn't help at all. I got tagged out before I got to base, and John said I kick like a girl, and everyone laughed. He's right. I'm an awful kicker. But John and his whole gang kept calling me Danielle and saying I was a girl, and saying "Poor Danielle has a fuss" and "Don't fuss, Hasenfuss!" And then when they picked teams for a second game Marco and Drew picked the girls before they picked me. I hate PE and I hate kickball and I hate John and I hate the whole stupid class!

Anyway, I hope you're okay. Are you kidding about the professor and the politician and Dad being called a frog-face? Dad says you're exaggerating again, but I believe you. Anyway, I believe mean enough words can hurt you that badly. I felt like I was getting punched in the solar plexus all through PE today. (I looked it up, so I know.)

Say hi to Napoleon for me.

- Danny

From: melbahasenfuss@another.com
Subject: **Re: I hate PE!**
Date: Wednesday, October 14, 9:53 PM
To: dhasenfuss@something.com

My dear Danny,

I'm very sorry to hear that you had such an unpleasant time in PE today, but I must beg you to give a little thought to what you're telling me. This John fellow obviously thinks nothing could be worse and more degrading than to be like a girl, and you appear to agree with him. You complain of this to me, a genuine female for the entirety of my extensive life? (Moreover, I've always been 100% satisfied with being a girl.) In your rush to consider yourself the victim you've lost sight of the feelings of others. How do you think the girls in your class feel when you boys use "girl" as a term of contempt? By accepting "girl" as an insult, you yourself insult any girls who hear it. Secondly, if the team captains picked girls before they picked you, that may imply that you're less than a star kickball player, but doesn't it equally imply that at least some of these girls they picked must be creditable players themselves?

"Kicking like a girl" is not necessarily such a bad thing – nor, indeed, is kicking like your Grandma. It wasn't so long ago that I had occasion to demonstrate that, and it's a shame you weren't there to see it for your edification. Last Fourth of July they had a swing band playing in the bandstand in the evening before the fireworks started, and everyone was dancing. I can still cut quite a rug, and I was dancing up a storm. Then all of a sudden there was a commotion where the fireworks were being set up. Some idiot had been smoking and threw a cigarette butt over near the fireworks and started one of the fuses. Even worse than that, the release mechanism hadn't been completed and the firework was about to detonate right on the ground with all sorts of people around. And of course it would probably set off all the other fireworks, too, and cause a dreadful explosion. The firemen were over at the hotdog stand getting their dinner before the fireworks were supposed to start, and there wasn't time for them to get back. So I didn't waste a second. I took careful aim, (in perfect time to the jitterbug, I might add), drew back my leg and kicked. I kicked off my shoe and it flew straight at the fireworks cannon and smacked into the release catch precisely as I had aimed. The release catch released just as the flame reached the end of the fuse, the cannon fired, the firework shot safely into the sky where it belonged, everyone cried, "Ooooh!" and "Aaaah!" and the day, or rather the evening, was saved. All because of a girl's kick. Let this be a lesson to you!

(Alas, my shoe was shot into the air with the firework and ended its dancing career in a blaze of glory. But, as you know, I'm never without a crochet hook in my hair bun, and I was able to whip up a replacement slipper for myself so that at least I didn't have to spend the rest of the evening dancing with one bare foot.)

I'm sorry to scold you, my dear, because you're my absolute favorite grandson, and not bad for a boy. In any case, we can't have you being bullied, so we need a new strategy. If lying low is impossible, perhaps you should try replying calmly and reasonably to John's calumnies. (See, I can use your vocabulary words, too.) Please remember, however, before you complain of insults, to think who else is being insulted by your attitude, and try respecting them.

Yours most affectionately, Grandma

From: dhasenfuss@something.com
Subject: **Help! It's getting worse!**
Date: Thursday, October 15, 8:33 PM
To: melbahasenfuss@another.com

Hi Grandma,

I didn't mean that girls are bad. Sorry if I offended you. I wish I had been there to see your awesome kick! And you're right about some of the girls being decent kickball players. I wish I were half as good as Hannah! But I don't think your advice worked out too well. In the hall before math today John and Connor came up behind me going, "Oh look, it's Danielle!" Brandon and Drew guffawed like they always do, and Austin shoved into me and made me drop my math book, and Connor said, "Oh, the poor little girl dropped her book."

So I tried to follow your advice and I answered, "There's nothing wrong with girls. I'd rather be a girl than be a boy like you. And Hannah's a lot better at kickball than Brandon and Drew, anyway." Hannah and Madison were there, too, by that time, and they frowned when I said that, and went into class whispering to each other, so I don't think they appreciated it. So I hope you do, Grandma! Because then it got even worse!

When I leaned over to pick up the book, one of those guys pushed me, and I stumbled forward and ran right into Mr Zangway, who was just coming to the door to see what was going on. I crashed into him and knocked him over! Then Rasheed, who was getting a drink from the water fountain in the hall, laughed so hard he squirted water out his nose all over the floor. This loser Kyle, who's always late to class, came dashing up just then because the bell was about to ring, and he slipped on the wet floor and went skidding down the hall, and his books and pencils flew up in the air and he crashed into two seventh graders at the door of their classroom. By that time everyone was laughing pretty hard, including me, but of course Mr Zangway was kind of mad, and when he yelled at everyone, John whispered sarcastically, "Way to go,

11

Fussy-fuss. 100% on your vocab quizzes and always so cool, too," and the whole gang snickered again and said "Don't fuss, Hasenfuss!" and stupid stuff like that. So your advice didn't help anything. I think I either need to get better at kickball or get worse grades!

By the way, we're about to start a unit on advertising in social studies and I'm supposed to collect different kinds of ads. Can you send me some ads out of some of your magazines? Dad's magazines are boring and have only the same sort of ads over and over, like banks and cars.

  - Danny

From: melbahasenfuss@another.com
Subject: **Re: Help! It's getting worse!**
Date: Thursday, October 15, 9:27 PM
To: dhasenfuss@something.com

Dear Danny,

I shall certainly select some interesting advertisements from my magazines and get them into the mail to you right away. If you have any particular subjects or styles in mind, let me know.

There are several points of note in your narrative, but I'm in a hurry tonight as I have to leave in just a few minutes for a performance. I just got a call from a friend of mine in the house band at Carnegie's that their trombonist had an unexpected and tragic toothbrushing accident and they need me to fill in. I'm afraid I'm a little rusty, but I dare say I'll play well enough to please people who are busily eating their dinners and talking the whole time anyway. But I do need to change my clothes and dump the cat out of the trombone as soon as I finish this note to you, so I'll say only that I'm sorry you felt that school today was worse than ever. If the bullying has progressed from name-calling to pushing and shoving we must certainly find a way to put a stop to it without further ado.

Just remember, if you must improve at kickball, that can do no harm, but under no circumstances attempt to become worse at spelling or your other schoolwork. However much John and his henchmen tease you for academic prowess, I assure you that bad grades will provide no respite from your troubles. There are as many cruel names for poor students as there are for good ones.

Hastily yours, Grandma

From: dhasenfuss@something.com
Subject: **bad vocab quiz**
Date: Friday, October 16, 7:39 PM
To: melbahasenfuss@another.com

Hi Grandma,

How did your gig go? What was Napoleon doing in your trombone anyway? I hope you played well.

I was only kidding about getting worse grades and I didn't mean to flunk my vocab quiz, but those guys were messing me up again today! During English they were teasing me every chance they got. Austin, who was sitting behind me, kept poking me with his pencil and I was getting totally distracted. And he kept whispering stuff during the quiz so I couldn't concentrate. Finally I whispered "Shut up!" and of course Ms Tulip heard me and said, "Austin and Dan, you know there is no talking permitted during a quiz. You will both get zeros until you come after school and retake the quiz." I was so mad! And of course then John and the others just made fun of both of us for being stupid, so you were at least right about that, Grandma!

So I had to come after school and I just wanted to retake the stupid quiz and get out of there, but Ms Tulip made me and Austin quiz each other on the vocab words. Man, he's terrible! I mean, I knew Austin got pretty bad grades, but I had no idea what a terrible speller he is. I didn't want to give him any help at all, but Ms Tulip sat at her desk looking daggers at me with one eyebrow raised whenever I wasn't helpful enough. So we quizzed each other through clenched teeth, and of course it was mostly me having to quiz him, totally ticked off the whole time. Then finally she let us retake the quiz, and I got 100%, but I only get a grade of 80% because it was a retake, and Austin got 81% to begin with, which means 61% with the markdown.

But this is the kicker - I was seriously annoyed about the whole thing and packing up my backpack and heading out, when Austin came up behind me. I figured he would probably poke me with the pencil again, or shove me or something, so I kind of hunched my shoulders and braced myself. And he did go shoving by me, but as he did he whispered, "Thanks for the help, Dan. 81%'s the best I ever scored on a vocab quiz." Can you believe it? I can't believe I helped one of that horrible gang! Man, I'm such a loser I help them after they ruin my grades! And we have a science lab test on Monday and I bet Rasheed's going to ruin that one for me, too. One thing's for sure, though, I'm going to study this weekend until my head explodes if I have to, to make up for having him for a lab partner.

      - Danny

Here are the new vocab words for this week: amuck, brandish, commotion, flourish, sheepish, skulk

From: melbahasenfuss@another.com
Subject: **Re: bad vocab quiz**
Date: Friday, October 16, 10:06 PM
To: dhasenfuss@something.com

My dear Danny,
      It is indeed frustrating to have your vocabulary quiz
spoiled by someone else's misbehavior. How infuriating to
have to go after school, and not get full credit for your
answers, either! However, I'm not so sure that helping
Austin was a bad thing. You may find that he won't look
at you in quite the same light any more, and perhaps you
might look at him in a different light, as well.
      Now let me tell you about my gig. First you should
know that Napoleon has taken to curling up in the bell of
my trombone and napping there, I don't know why.
Perhaps the metal warms up in the sunlight or something.
At any rate, every time I want to play I have to dump him
out first. So between that and changing my clothes and
catching the subway to Carnegie's I barely made it in time,
and the first set started immediately upon my arrival.
That meant I didn't take the time to warm up properly
before we began. The music started, I took a big breath
and belted out my first notes... only it turned out that
Napoleon had left a fair amount of fur in my trombone,
and the fur went flying out and into the face of the
woman at the first table below the stage. Well, apparently
she was extremely allergic to cats and within seconds she
had begun to sneeze hard enough to double her over...
which was a good thing, because some utterly abysmal
fool had brought a loaded gun into Carnegie's and
managed to bang it against the edge of a table so it went
off! It shot straight across the front of the room and
would have hit the woman in front and almost certainly
killed her if she hadn't happened to lean forward at just
that instant with another tremendous Napoleon-fur-
induced sneeze. The security guards were on top of the

16

idiot with the gun by the time the bullet ricocheted off the cymbal and struck the emergency exit sign stage right. That popped and fizzled sparks on the percussionist's head, but he appeared to notice neither that nor the dent in his cymbal, and kept right on playing while the audience went into fits. They were far too busy panicking to pay any attention to my first solo, but that may have been just as well since, as I told you, I was a little rusty. With the near exit light out of order they all ran helter-skelter back toward the main entrance, where the bouncers could assure them that the man with the gun was already ejected. So luckily everything soon settled back down, because as you know I don't care for such disturbances, and the set continued without further incident.

By the time I'd packed up and left Carnegie's for the subway station afterwards, it was well after midnight and most of the audience was already gone. The streets were pretty deserted and there was only one man, and it seemed like he was following me. And then I realized that I recognized him – it was the fool who'd almost shot the woman in Carnegie's - so then I knew he had a gun! I confess it made me a little nervous to know he was coming up closer and closer behind me with nobody else around. I don't know what a mugger would want with a trombone, but of course muggers can like jazz, too, and anyway, I thought he probably assumed I had a lot of money with me.

But less than a block from the subway station he suddenly lurched forward and fell on his face. At first I considered ignoring him, but after all, he hadn't tried mugging me yet, and maybe he wasn't really planning to at all. So I turned around to see what was the matter. He was lying on the ground clutching his ankle and moaning. Apparently he'd caught his toe on a crack in the sidewalk and twisted his ankle pretty badly. Well, I couldn't just leave the poor bloke all alone in a sketchy part of town late at night with a twisted ankle, so I went back to help him. He said he lived about half a block away and if he could just get home he'd be okay. I tried to offer him a shoulder, but he was too heavy for me, so after a little thought I let him use my trombone (in its case, of course) as a sort of crutch. I hated to see my poor case getting banged against the sidewalk, but after all, what are a few scuffs as long as the trombone is perfectly safe inside? When we reached his building he said, "Let me get my cousin to walk you to the station. It's not safe around here."

So the cousin came down to escort me to the subway station. He introduced himself as Tony and said, "You know an old lady like you shouldn't be walking around here alone."

I replied, "But I wasn't alone. Your cousin was right behind me."

He gave me a funny look and said, "Lady, my cousin is exactly the kind of dude I'm trying to warn you about!"

I nodded and said, "Ah yes, I thought he might be a mugger."

"Then why'd you help him?" he exclaimed.

"Because he'd hurt his ankle, of course!"

At that Tony laughed and said, "Well, maybe you're pretty smart or maybe you're just lucky, but either way I guess you're all right. Here's the station." I thanked him and he replied, "Thanks for helping my cousin. Maybe he'll remember it next time he's thinking of going out with that gun. He's really not all bad." What do you think of that?

As for the challenge of your upcoming lab test, no doubt you're right to study as if you'll have to do everything on your own. As everyone always says, if you want something done right, you have to do it yourself, and if your lab partner is as bad as you say, he'll be no help at all. However, you're an excellent student and I'm sure you can handle it, my dear!

Yours affectionately, Grandma

From: dhasenfuss@something.com
Subject: **soccer game**
Date: Saturday, October 17, 5:28 PM
To: melbahasenfuss@another.com

Hi Grandma,

It's not fair - I can't escape from John's gang even on the weekend! My friend Eric came over this afternoon and his sister's soccer team had a game, and he wanted to go over and watch for a while. So we biked over to the field when there was about 20 minutes left in the game. Well, it turns out John's friend Hannah is on the same team as Eric's sister, so John and a couple of the other guys and Madison were all there to watch, too. Eric and I climbed up the side of the bleacher to the top row and John didn't notice us at first. Our side was down 2-1 and we kept getting close, but just couldn't seem to score. Then Eric's sister got the ball and he started cheering her on, and that's when John and all those guys turned around and saw us.

I'm sure they would have said something mean anyway, but just then this bee started buzzing around. Eric's allergic to bees and he totally freaked out. All of a sudden he started screaming and jumping around and waving his arms like crazy and the next thing I knew, he flailed his arms into my face and knocked me over backwards, and I fell straight off the back of the bleachers! Of course by then John and every single other person at the game was staring at Eric the spaz, and everyone saw me flip right off the back like a total loser, and all the breath got knocked out of me, and John's gang was laughing their stupid heads off. I was so embarrassed I thought I'd die. And then everyone started cheering! I thought they were cheering because I fell! But when I picked myself up and climbed back onto the bleacher, Eric explained that our commotion had totally distracted the other team and in fact it had distracted everyone except his sister, who of course was used to ignoring him. And while no one was paying attention she was able to score a goal and tie the game!

By now there was only about 2 minutes left and John turned around and said, "Maybe if we push weenie Danielle off again we'll win the game!" Ha ha. But when his back was turned to sneer at me, Hannah made this kick that must have been about as good as yours at the fireworks! She scored, and we won! So that was good. But Eric went home with his family, and I had to bike home all bruised and sore. Ugh.

Just as I got home, Hannah came biking by and believe it or not, she stopped and asked if I was okay. So I said yeah I was fine, and then I said what an awesome score she made, and she grinned and said, "Maybe a bit better than Brandon and Drew, huh?"

I laughed sort of sheepishly, because she was obviously remembering what I said before math class the other day. Then she surprised me even more by saying, "Look, Dan, you want to kick better?" and she got off her bike and pulled a soccer ball out of her backpack and gave me a few pointers! So then I went in the back yard and practiced what she said for a little while before dinner, and I really do think I was doing better!

So maybe there's hope for me yet, Grandma. And I must admit it seems you may have been right about sticking up for girls. Hannah's never said two words to me before, so even if your advice just made things worse with John, I think it really helped with Hannah, anyway. But as for John, I bet he'll be teasing me worse than ever for falling off the bleacher, so if you have any more ideas for dealing with him, go ahead and tell me!
　　　　- Danny

From: melbahasenfuss@another.com
Subject: **Re: soccer game**
Date: Saturday, October 17, 8:41 PM
To: dhasenfuss@something.com

My dear Danny,

How gratifying to hear that my advice may have done some good! And how nice also to hear that one girl, at least, thinks of something more than giggling about clothes. Congratulations on your improved kicking abilities, and I trust that you've recovered fully from your tumble at the game. As for advice on dealing with the abhorrent John, perhaps you could take your cue from your dealings with Hannah. Look how she's responded to kindness, and consider whether such a strategy might not work equally well with John. As always, please let me know all your news.

As for my news, I spent a quiet Saturday patching and polishing my trombone case and trying to clear the cat hair from the valves. I think I'll have to lay a cloth across it from now on to keep Napoleon's napping habit from causing any more problems. I've also been collecting magazine advertisements for you as you requested, and I sent a packet of them off to you this morning. Let me know if they're what you needed or if I should look for anything else.

Yours fondly, Grandma

From: dhasenfuss@something.com
Subject: **gossip about the sewer rat**
Date: Sunday, October 18, 1:55 PM
To: melbahasenfuss@another.com

Hi Grandma,

Remember Connor, one of John's gang? He's the one who looks like a sewer rat, always skulking around in the background looking mean and nervous at the same time. Well, Dad said he heard at church today that Connor's parents are getting a divorce, and Connor's dad is in trouble for something at his job, like not getting the right permits or something, and the police are investigating him! So you can see the whole family's rotten, I guess! Next time Connor says something mean to me I'll just mention something about his dad and I bet that will shut him up! I can't wait to see his face.

I'm going to spend the rest of today studying like crazy for tomorrow's lab test. I'm not going to let that gang spoil any more grades for me!

Thanks for sending the ads. I'll tell you if I need any more after I see them.

Can't you just leave the lid shut on the trombone case and not let Napoleon sleep in the bell part any more?
    - Danny

From: melbahasenfuss@another.com
Subject: **Re: gossip about the sewer rat**
Date: Sunday, October 18, 7:08 PM
To: dhasenfuss@something.com

My dearest Danny,

Yes, of course I could close the case, but you know how I am about just picking up my trombone and playing any old time. Besides, why deprive Napoleon of his happy place? It's one of his endearing habits. Although I admit that whenever I see him snoozing there in the trombone there's a strong temptation to tiptoe up and blast as hard as I can and see how far he flies. To date, however, I've restrained myself.

I can't write any more tonight as I've gotten dreadfully behind on my needlepoint. I'm supposed to have three more pillow covers made before the benefit auction next week and it's going to be quite a job to finish. I would have had only two more to go, except that I don't think anyone will want to buy the one with the singe marks on it from the lightning.

I hope your studying has gone well today and you feel confident about the test. Good luck!

Busily yours, Grandma

From: dhasenfuss@something.com
Subject: **lab test**
Date: Monday, October 19, 8:12 PM
To: melbahasenfuss@another.com

Hey Grandma,

You'll never believe how the lab test turned out! I was cramming until the very last second, and then when the test started I jumped right in to do everything like we planned. I fetched all the materials from the supply shelves, I laid out all the equipment, I prepared all the stuff myself.

Rasheed tried to do some of it at first, but I sort of ignored him and kept right on going, and after a while he just stood there with his arms crossed, scowling at me. But meanwhile the whole time John and Drew, who were at the next table over, were trying to do whatever they could to mess me up. They stuck out their feet when I walked past, they joggled my elbows, they whispered all kinds of jokes about me falling off the bleacher and stuff. I tried to stay focused, but I couldn't help getting flustered, and the more they bugged me the more trouble I was having concentrating. It was slowing me down, and I was running out of time, and that was getting me even more flustered!

Finally I was ready to mix the five solutions that Ms Diaz was going to grade and just as I was about to add some chlorine, Rasheed smacked my hand away and hissed "No!" I thought he'd managed to ruin everything for me again! I was so mad I didn't even know what to say for a second, but then he whispered, "You can't do that, Dan. It'll make poison gas." And I looked at what I was doing, and I remembered all that stuff I studied, and I saw that he was right! Then he whispered, "You're supposed to add this one. And only 5 ml, not 50." I was still so surprised I was just staring at him, so he took the ingredients and started mixing them himself. And he did everything exactly right! He scowled at me and growled, "Come on! I don't have enough time left to do this all

24

myself!" So I kind of pulled myself together, and started helping him, but by that time I was so flustered I hardly knew what I was doing and Rasheed gave me instructions on everything! And we finished our last solution just in time, and Ms Diaz gave us 96%, and it was all because of Rasheed!

I was so relieved that when we were cleaning up our lab station I gave him a huge grin, but he just scowled and looked like a big mean Doberman dog as usual, and whispered, "Don't say a word about this to anyone! If you dare tell John or any of the others, I will crush you. Get it?"

I sputtered, "Are you insane? I bet you're the best student in science class! Why would you keep that a secret?"

He snarled, "I don't want those guys thinking I'm some wimpy loser nerd like you, that's why!"

My brains must have been totally scrambled from the whole experience, because instead of shutting up like any smart kid would have done at that point, I just shook my head and said, "That's stupid, Rasheed!" (I can't believe I called Rasheed stupid to his face!) He cracked his knuckles at me, so I quick added, "I won't tell anyone if you don't want, but I don't get it. You're way smarter than those guys, and you're just as tough as them, too, so why do you care what they think? They'd never push you around like they do me."

Just then the bell rang and we left to our next classes, but what do you think of that, Grandma? I wish I'd asked Rasheed how he knew all that stuff, because he sure doesn't look like he ever pays any attention in class! But I'd better not, because he'll probably beat me up if I ever mention it. Anyway, I got my best grade ever on a science test because of him! Of course, I would've done fine on my own if all his stupid friends hadn't messed me up in the first place, so I guess I still need a solution to that problem. Any more advice for me?
- Danny

From: melbahasenfuss@another.com
Subject: **Re: lab test**
Date: Monday, October 19, 10:24 PM
To: dhasenfuss@something.com

Dear Danny,

Congratulations on your excellent science test grade! It's always so fascinating to find out you've been wrong about someone. But why not ask Rasheed about his hidden science skill? As long as you do so during some private moment when his "friends" can't hear, I suspect he'd be happy to have the opportunity to talk about a subject which he's obviously been unable to discuss with anyone before. And as for my advice regarding John, that seems quite obvious: try a little kindness and see whether that doesn't turn him around as it already has for Hannah and perhaps some others. Is there some little generosity you could extend to him that would take him by surprise and make him rethink his attitude toward you?

My own life is quite boring at the moment, but you know that's fine with me, since I always enjoy the quiet life. Needlepoint needlepoint needlepoint. There was just a little excitement this morning when I wasn't paying enough attention and embroidered the tip of Napoleon's tail right onto one of my pillow covers. The design was of a black cat just like Napoleon, so I didn't notice at the time that his tail fur was mixed in with my stitches.

He didn't notice at the time, either, but when he woke from his nap and hopped down from the loveseat beside me, and the cushion cover yanked out of my hands and came down after him, it startled us both dreadfully and he whirled around in a fright. Of course the pillow cover whirled around behind him, and I'm afraid the poor creature rather panicked. He started bolting around the room, but the pillow cover dragged around after him, and he spun and thrashed, but the pillow cover spun and thrashed with him, and he yowled and spat (which the pillow cover did not do), and he tore across my desk and knocked over the lamp, which came down with a tremendous crash that made him panic all the more, so he leaped up and tried to hide in my trombone with the pillow cover still attached. With his head stuffed well down into the trombone he calmed down enough that I could pick his tail out of the needlepoint. I'm afraid I'll need another new shade and bulb for my desk lamp, but these things happen, and luckily I think the cushion will still be saleable, because I have only six days to finish it and another after it, and with any more excitement I'll never get them done. In fact, I'd better get back to work right now!

Yours affectionately, Grandma

From: dhasenfuss@something.com
Subject: **another crazy day**
Date: Tuesday, October 20, 4:52 PM
To: melbahasenfuss@another.com

Hi Grandma,

I don't know about this whole kindness strategy. All it seems to have gotten me is another totally crazy day, and more trouble from John. See, I decided I'd give him a package of Swedish fish, since those are my favorites and I was trying to do unto him as I wish people would do unto me more often, which is how Dad said you're supposed to do it. I figured if I was going to go out on a limb, I might as well really do it right. I wrote a note that said, "I know you don't like me too much, but I hope you have a good day anyway." Embarrassingly corny, I know, but it's hard to be nice without being corny, and like I said, I figured there was no point in doing it halfway. When I got to first period, John and a couple of the others were already there, so I waited until the loser Kyle came scampering in late making a big commotion like he always does, and while everybody was laughing at him I sneakily stuck the Swedish fish into John's backpack. Then I sat back to see what would happen.

Well, maybe this was a bad day to try out the plan, because John seemed to be in an all-time world-record mean mood today. First of all he fired off a whole string of nasty remarks about Kyle, and then he was hard at work teasing me, and to top it off he was being a creep to half his own friends, too. Especially Connor. In fact, he was saying to Connor all the things I'd thought of saying to him myself, about how his dad's a pathetic crook and no wonder his mother wants to leave and the whole family is a bunch of losers, and all that sort of stuff. And I have to admit that with John saying it, it sounded really really mean, so I'm kind of glad I didn't get a chance to say it. I mean, I actually started feeling kind of sorry for Connor, if you can believe it, Grandma! His eyes got sort of red all around and about ten minutes into class he just suddenly

28

exploded, "Shut up, John!" and of course Ms Quam got mad at him. But at least she moved his seat "away from his friends," which I'm sure he was happy about by then.

Then later when I went in to third period, I had to pass John and Connor talking at the door, and Connor was saying something sappy about how John was a true friend after all, and John was looking at him with the look he usually gives me, which is probably the same look he gives a piece of moldy liver, and he was saying, "I don't know what you're talking about, Convict – I mean Connor - but if you think I'd be making nice to a loser like you, you're even more pathetic than I thought." Then John shoved past me and Eric with a "Get lost, Danielle. And get a new sweatshirt, while you're at it," and then Kyle came dashing up losing papers and pencils all over the place, and class began.

Class stank. We were in small groups to do the project, and do I get to be in a group with Eric or any of the decent kids? No. Of course I got stuck with John, Drew, and Brandon as my group, and they were being meaner than ever. Why me, Grandma? Seriously, how can I possibly be so unlucky, out of everyone in the entire class? But anyway finally I said, "Jeez, John, what's wrong with you after I even tried to be nice to you!" And he looked at me like I was psycho (and Brandon and Drew started tittering) and said, "You tried to be nice? As if you could possibly do anything for me that I would care about. I think Fussy-fuss Danielle has finally lost it completely." Then Brandon said "Ooo, Danielle trying to be nice to John?" and Drew started singing, "Danielle loves John, Danielle loves John!"

Thank goodness just then our group got called to go up and present the poster we'd made, so they couldn't very well keep tormenting me in front of the entire class and the teacher and all. But you can imagine what I was thinking of your kindness strategy by then, Grandma! The absolute worst most horrible failure ever, that's what!

Okay, but then things got weird. When I went to the bathroom on the way to lunch Connor was in there wiping his face as if he'd been crying. Like I said, I felt kind of sorry for him by then, so I asked if he was okay, and he kind of gulped and nodded and stared at me like a sick puppy. Which was sort of weird to begin with. Then in the cafeteria John tried to trip me when I went past with my tray. That's not weird. He does that sort of thing all the time. At least I didn't fall over and drop the whole thing, but my French fries skidded off the tray and scattered all over the floor. So of course John and Drew, Brandon, Marco, and Madison all started laughing at me, and the lunch lady came stomping over and yelled, "Who threw these fries?"

John put on his kissing-up face and said, "Dan did it, Mrs Guglielmo. He was trying to put them down my shirt!" Of course I denied it and explained that John had tried to trip me, but Mrs Guglielmo brandished her ladle and ordered, "Dan Hasenfuss, you get down on your knees and pick up these fries!" Before I had time to protest, Connor jumped up so fast he knocked over his own fries, and with this totally crazed look on his face he blurted out, "No! It was John's fault, just like Dan said! John's a dirty mean liar and you should never believe a word he says! Dan's a better person than you'll ever be, John, and *you're* the pathetic loser for trying to push him down because you wouldn't know how to be a decent person if your life depended on it!" And then he gulped and bolted out of the cafeteria!

Everyone just stared, totally astonished and kind of embarrassed, too, and Marco said "What the *%#@!" and then all of a sudden the lunch lady burst into tears!!! "That was so beautiful!" she sobbed, "Just like all those wonderful movies back in the 80's. I loved those movies! True friends always stand up for each other in the end, and the bullies always get a come-down!"

John said in a snarky voice, "Woah! Mrs Guglielmo, as you know Connor's been a friend of mine for a long time, so I'm sorry to have to tell you that he's got some, um, issues. Maybe you don't know that he's in counseling for his pathological lying problem and emotional outbursts." He smirked around at his friends.

But the lunch lady smacked his tray with her ladle so hard that the milk carton bounced two inches into the air and she bellowed, "You got a problem with emotional outbursts?" Her face was purple and her eyes were still streaming tears, so John realized he'd made a mistake. "Of course not, Mrs Guglielmo!" he said quickly, "Emotional outbursts are very healthy! But I just wanted you to understand that you can't believe anything poor Connor says!" But she crossed her arms and snapped, "Get down on that floor and pick up these French fries, John Marshall! RIGHT NOW! And you can help him, Dan." Well, I didn't want to argue with a two-ton woman wielding a lethal ladle and still snuffling about old movies, so I picked up the French fries with John while Mrs Guglielmo stood over us with the ladle and babbled on in a dreamy voice, "I always wanted to be in one of those movies. Everyone used to say I looked just like Molly Ringwald." So then she started gazing into the distance and making these flourishes and gestures like she was before a crowd of adoring fans or something.

John muttered to his friends, "Oh my god, the lunch lady's just as crazy as Convict Connor! Maybe she can be his new mother since his dad'll be in jail and his mom probably can't wait to get away from him." Some of his gang snickered, but Austin said, "Aw, give him a break. I thought he was our friend."

The lunch lady must have heard the word "friend," because she sighed dramatically, "Isn't friendship beautiful!" and made a big sweeping gesture - and the ladle flew out of her hand and right across the lunchroom, and through the window with a crash! And from outside we heard a string of terrible curses in a voice that was unmistakably the principal's! And then we heard "Get this #*@% thing away from me!" and a second later the ladle came shooting back through the window, straight down into the middle of John's tray like a meteor, and bounced his French fries all over his head and onto the floor. Marco let loose a few more swearwords, but Mrs Guglielmo just said, "Oh dear! Sorry!" with a cheerful giggle. Then she looked down at John all speckled with splattered ketchup and said, "You really should do something for that acne, dear."

By then everyone on that side of the cafeteria was falling out of their chairs laughing. John just gave me the world's most evil look and hissed, "Connor's the one who got me into this mess, but you'd better believe one thing, weenie Danielle. If I ever find out you had anything to do with Connor blabbing, I'll make you sorry you were ever born!"

I didn't say anything, but grabbed my tray and rushed over to sit with Eric at the opposite end of the cafeteria before anything else could happen! Of course Eric wanted to know what it was all about, and after I filled him in I said, "You think we ought to go check if Connor's all right?" Eric said, "You know, I hate to say this, but John might be right. What if all the pressure really drove Connor insane? He sounds a little unstable, and you know something else? When you guys presented your poster in social studies, he asked me if it was your handwriting on it. Isn't that weird? And when I said it was, he was like "Oh my god, I can't believe it!" like it was this big important deal, and he was all muttering to himself and getting teary-eyed and stuff. Does that sound normal to you?" It sure didn't sound normal to me, and then Eric goes "Oh my god, what if he really loses it and tries to kill himself or something!" So we decided we'd better go check if he was in the bathroom.

We went out and sure enough he was in there, and when he saw us he burst into tears!!! And he started going on about how sorry he was he'd ever been mean to me, and he never realized what a great person I was and he was going through a really hard time at home right now and it meant so much to him to have someone be so thoughtful, especially since he'd thought John was his friend and now it turned out he wasn't, and on and on.

Eric and I thought he was completely psycho because it wasn't like we were being all that nice (although I guess compared to John just about anyone else seems like an angel.) We thought he really had gone kind of insane and we were trying to get him to go see the nurse or the

32

advisor or something. But then he sniffled and wiped his nose and sort of calmed down and said, "No, thanks. I'm okay. It just sort of hit me, when I really needed a friend to have John turn on me and then to have you give me those Swedish fish. How did you know they're my favorite?" And then I realized that by mistake I must have slipped them into Connor's backpack instead of John's!!!!!

Eric thought Connor was even more totally insane at that point, because I'd been too embarrassed to tell Eric about the kindness strategy. So I managed to stutter out something about how I didn't know, but they're my favorite, too, and then the bell rang for the end of lunch. Wow! Connor said, "Well, I'm just really sorry it took me this long to realize who the good guys at this school are. Thanks, dude." And then we went to class.

So there it is, Grandma! Your advice was a total fiasco! Even if it sort of worked with Connor, John's bound to find out about the Swedish fish, and then he'll blame me for Connor telling on him at lunch, and then he'll kill me! Help!

      - Danny

From: melbahasenfuss@another.com
Subject: **Re: another crazy day**
Date: Tuesday, October 20, 10:16 PM
To: dhasenfuss@something.com

Dear Danny,

My goodness, what an interesting day for you! But I must say that it doesn't sound like a total fiasco to me. I'd call it a definite collateral success. But I can understand your concern about John's vengeance, and he does sound as if kindness is having difficulty getting through to him. In such situations as these it's certainly tempting to consider violence - perhaps throwing a particularly heavy book at his head, for example! But I'll have to give the matter more thought, and I'm confident that we can overcome this conflict eventually.

There's not much news here, except needlepoint needlepoint needlepoint.

Napoleon dashed out the window early this morning when I opened it to shake out my dust cloth. Stupid beast. He'd never stand a chance in the wild, especially not with this pack of feral dogs we've had around recently. But, like his namesake, he seems to think he's the biggest thing in town. I had to go out on the fire escape after him and he had the nerve to look affronted when I fetched him back inside. He jumped straight into my trombone and sulked. He's just lucky I know some mountaineering, otherwise I'd never have been able to get to him without falling to my death, and then who would feed him? As it was I had to loop my bathrobe tie around the railing and rappel down to reach him. Thank goodness Mr Montague downstairs didn't see me dangling outside his window in my nightgown, as he'd be sure to think it was flirtation and he's far too eager as it is. But he didn't see, and the stupid cat was recovered, and we all survived to tell the tale. And I hope you survive PE tomorrow!

Yours affectionately, Grandma

From: dhasenfuss@something.com
Subject: **crazy kickball!**
Date: Wednesday, October 21, 7:34 PM
To: melbahasenfuss@another.com

Hey Grandma,

You shouldn't call Napoleon stupid! He's awesome. Give him a pet for me! But I'm glad you got him back safely.

Well, I survived PE today, but it was certainly interesting! You aren't going to believe everything that happened, Grandma! The first astonishing thing was that Hannah picked me for her team! Pretty early, too, even before John got picked, and he said all snarky, "I guess you want all the girls on your team, huh, Hannah!" But she just grinned and said "Let's hear it for girl power!" and although that was kind of embarrassing, she gave me a wink that was actually nice, not mean! So then when I first came up to bat, there were kids on third and first and Hannah whispered "Kick it to Drew. He won't catch it." So like she said I kicked it to Drew in the infield, and sure enough just like she said, he dropped it, and I got to first and the kid on third came home for a score! I've never had my kickball team cheering for me before! But unfortunately we got three outs before I got a chance to try to make it home.

Okay, so that was really cool, but then the second time I came up to bat John was pitching for the other team. He gave me this mean smile, and whipped the ball right at my head! Hannah said I should just let him keep doing it and he'd end up walking me, but I remembered your advice about using violence, so the next time he pitched I just kicked the ball the hardest I've ever kicked in my life, straight back at his head. It wacked him right in the forehead, which was about my best aim ever, but I didn't get a chance to feel too smug about it, because the ball bounced right back straight at me, and wacked *me* right in the eye. John and I were both knocked over, and John had a red spot on his forehead, but my eye started swelling up and turning purple right away, so Mr Viggles sent me to the nurse to get an ice pack.

Well, when I got to the nurse, John's buddy Marco was there sitting on a cot with an ice pack on his left ankle. His shoe and pants were sopping wet up to the calf and he had a scrape all up his shin, and the nurse was telling him he could borrow some crutches for the rest of the day. When I asked what happened, Marco turned red as a kickball.

"What happened to *you*?" he demanded. Well, I was pretty embarrassed to tell him, but I knew John and the others would tell him later anyway, so I explained how the ball bounced off John's head and came back and hit me. Marco laughed, but when I asked him again what happened to him, he looked all sullen. But finally he sort of shrugged and muttered the story. Apparently he somehow got himself locked in the toilet stall, and since the floor was pretty dirty he didn't want to crawl out under the door. So he decided to climb over, instead. He climbed up onto the toilet, and was trying to swing a leg over the stall when his other foot slipped and went straight down into the toilet, banging his shin and twisting his ankle pretty badly. Of course I laughed at the thought of Marco standing there trapped in the bathroom stall with his foot down the toilet! So he growled, "I suppose you're gonna tell everybody now, aren't you, you $#@ little %&@*. I bet you'd think it would be funny to tell Hannah."
"Why Hannah?" I asked, and then I realized I bet Marco's got a crush on Hannah! He turned all red again and said, "You %*$@ weenie! You are gonna tell her, aren't you!"

Well, of course I had been planning to tell everyone, but when I thought about it I started feeling kinda bad about it. I mean, I knew John would tease him horribly even though they were friends, and it would be even more embarrassing to have the girls laughing at him, too, so on the spur of the moment I said I wouldn't tell. "Yeah, right," said Marco.

Now that made me kind of mad and I got all huffy and said, "I don't know about you, but when I say I won't do something, I won't do it!" And I tried to give him a sort of noble and trustworthy look. And for the first time he looked me straight in the eye – the one eye without the ice pack, that is - and said, "Thanks!" in this surprised voice. So I didn't tell anyone, not even Eric. (Well, I'm telling you, of course, Grandma, but I know you won't let the secret out at Edgar Middle School.)

The nurse made me carry his books to his next class for him, and when I dropped them off on his desk he gave me a sort of grin and said, "Man, I'm %#$* sorry I missed seeing you kick John in the #%@& head!" So, what do you think of that, Grandma? I guess you were right that violence was the best solution!

     - Danny

From: melbahasenfuss@another.com
Subject: **Re: crazy kickball!**
Date: Wednesday, October 21, 9:48 PM
To: dhasenfuss@something.com

My dear Danny,

I never suggested you use violence to solve your problems, and I'm sorry you should ever have thought I did! I said it was tempting to consider using violence, but I never for a moment meant for you to infer that it was the right course of action. Violence almost invariably rebounds upon its author in just the way you experienced – after all, it was you who ended up at the nurse's office with a puffy eye, and not John. However, I'm glad you feel that the episode was on the whole a positive one, and I hope your eye is fine now. You did indeed choose the noble path in keeping Marco's secret. It seems to me that a number of your classmates are ready to see you in a new light. Why not show them how worthy you are of popularity, instead of allowing them to cast you as the victim?

Napoleon sends a purr and appreciates your support of him.

Now I must get back to work on this needlepoint. I have to admit that as much as I enjoy my crafts, I'm getting quite bored with these interminable needlepoint pillows. As soon as I finish I'd like to try something completely different for a change. There are some very interesting patterns in some of my needlecraft magazines.

Fondly yours, Grandma

From: dhasenfuss@something.com
Subject: **helicopter cozy?**
Date: Thursday, October 22, 8:20 PM
To: melbahasenfuss@another.com

Hi Grandma,

Your magazine ads came today. Thanks! I think they'll be perfect for my assignment, and they're sure a lot more interesting than Dad's! But what kind of magazines do you read anyway, to have ads for "The world leader in survival crochet thread. The only crochet fiber strong enough to snare a charging rhino!" And I couldn't help but notice that on the back of the page there seemed to be part of the instructions for knitting a helicopter cozy! Is that the kind of "very interesting pattern" you're planning on trying next? Seriously, Grandma, have you really ever knitted a helicopter cozy or snared a rhino with crochet fiber? I thought you said you liked a quiet life.

I guess I misunderstood you about the violence, but luckily it worked out okay after all. And I think you're right that it's time for me to show them all that I can be cool instead of being the victim. There was the funniest incident today that had everyone laughing "with me not at me." At the lockers after lunch Kyle asked what time it was and I told him it was ten minutes earlier than it really was. You know how he's always late to everything? Well, so when everyone else was in class and the teacher had already started, he came strolling in through the door ten minutes late all pleased thinking he was on time for once. It was like he didn't even notice class had already begun. He walked right across the front of the room, right in front of Ms Tulip, who was standing at the whiteboard staring at him in the middle of writing out something about man vs man and man vs nature, with one eyebrow raised. Kyle waved at me, and called out "Hey, Zack!" to his friend, and plopped his books on his desk with a big clatter... So finally Ms Tulip says in that total teacher voice, "It's good of you to join us this afternoon, Kyle. Do let us know when you're quite ready for the rest of us to continue with our lesson." And Kyle looked around, and it's like he suddenly realized for the first time that he'd just walked into the middle of class, and he looked exactly like a balloon popping! His books fell out of his hands and he just drooped down into his chair with this look of utter disappointment - only he'd already pushed his chair aside, so he actually collapsed all the way down onto the floor in a heap, and everyone started laughing. But that's not all – on his way down he must have hit the edge of a notebook on the edge of the chair, and the notebook flipped up and catapulted his copy of "Treasure Island" up in the air, and it nearly hit the ceiling and when Kyle looked up with his mouth hanging open to see it, the book came back down right on his face! It was SOOOOO funny! People were falling out of their chairs laughing. Even John was laughing! It sure made a nice change not to be the one he was laughing at! (Especially since people have been laughing at my black eye all day.) And when Ms Tulip told Kyle he'd have to come in after school to make up the part of the lesson he missed, his face fell even farther and he cried, "But I can't stay after today! I have to take my hermit crab to the vet!" and everyone laughed even harder!

Ms Tulip said in full discipline voice, "That's enough, class! Kyle, you'll have to come in briefly, but perhaps we can arrange another time for you to make up the lesson. I'd hate to make it any harder for you to get to an appointment on time." That was really funny, too, but by then we didn't dare laugh any more because when Ms Tulip says "That's enough," we know she's serious. Anyway, the whole thing was hysterical! You should have seen it!

     - Danny

From: melbahasenfuss@another.com
Subject: **Re: helicopter cozy?**
Date: Thursday, October 22, 9:56 PM
To: dhasenfuss@something.com

My dearest Danny,

No, I have never knitted a helicopter cozy, silly boy. I don't even have a helicopter any more, of course! And you remind me of the old joke, "How can you tell when a rhino is getting ready to charge?" He takes out his credit card. I love that one. But believe it or not, "Auntie Jane's Hook-strong Technofloss" crochet thread is a product which I would never wish to be without. Just the other day I had occasion to use it. As you may have seen on the news about a month ago, a bear had been wandering into town and causing a terrible uproar. Mostly he went after people's garbage, but there had been a few dogs mauled, and people were all in a tizzy about safety and such. But after half an hour of quick work with the crochet needle (following the simple instructions in my *Adventure Needlecraft* magazine) I whipped up a drawstring net complete with trigger tripline. This I rigged above the trash collection area behind my building. At about five the next morning I heard a clatter and ran down to check on it, and sure enough I'd caught my bear. It was neatly bundled up in the net, gently swinging out of harm's way five feet off the ground, and all crocheted entirely from Technofloss. So while I've never actually snared a rhino with it, I can vouch for its efficacy with wild beasts in general. Anyway, I called animal control, and they transported the bear out to the state park, where I trust it's now living happily ever after. They asked to keep my net for future use. Threads, like words, can be more powerful than they seem.

As for your situation at school, I want to leave you with a simple question. What do you think Kyle's Grandma should advise him to do about you?

Yours thoughtfully, Grandma

From: dhasenfuss@something.com
Subject: **being nice to Kyle**
Date: Friday, October 23, 6:59 PM
To: melbahasenfuss@another.com

Hi Grandma,

I guess you mean that Kyle must think I was being as mean to him as John is to me. But it was just supposed to be a little joke, and anyway, why should I be the only one everyone always picks on? And if I'm a loser now, just imagine how much of a loser I'd be if I was friends with Kyle! You can't ask me to be nice to everybody.

Speaking of being nice, guess what happened at lunch today. Connor came over and asked to sit with me and Eric! I wasn't really sure I wanted to, but what can you say? And actually it turned out okay, except that when John went by he put ketchup French fries down my back and said he was helping me convince my parents to buy me new clothes because anything would be less dorky than what I had, (and Dad was all mad at me for getting a stain when he saw my shirt this evening), and of course the lunch lady didn't see a thing. She was probably too busy dreaming about being in the movies or something. And at the end Austin went by with his tray and looked like he was about to say something, or probably bang his tray on our heads or something, but just then a bunch of other kids came by, too, and he didn't do anything after all. Still, it made me sort of mad just to know he would have, so I guess I was feeling kind of cranky afterwards. I got 100% on my vocab, but in science we were supposed to be working on a lab project and I didn't really understand it and was having trouble and getting frustrated, and finally I got mad and said to Rasheed, "Come on, quit standing there looking too cool to work. You can probably do this stuff better than I can!"

I didn't know whether he was going to slug me for that, but after a quick glance over his shoulder to see that John wasn't paying any attention, he gave me a sort of embarrassed grin and started really joining in on the project. And it was actually pretty fun because he really helped me understand it better! Except then after a while John did notice, and he sneered, "Hey, Drew, looks like we have a couple of real geeks at the next table. Rasheed, I never knew you and Danielle Fussy-fuss the nerd had so much in common." So of course that set Rasheed back to scowling and cracking his knuckles and looking like a Doberman again. Still, at least he didn't say anything mean to me. And now it's the weekend, and hopefully I won't see any of that gang again for a couple of days. Yay! :) And maybe my eye will look normal again before next week.

And speaking of black eyes, "Treasure Island" must have landed on Kyle's eye yesterday, because it was sort of bruised and swollen today (but not nearly as bad as mine), and you know what's even funnier? Today we saw that Mr Budge (that's the principal) has an awful black eye (even worse than mine!) and we realized it must have been from the lunch lady's ladle on Tuesday!!!

Are you doing anything interesting this weekend?
- Danny

From: melbahasenfuss@another.com
Subject: **Re: being nice to Kyle**
Date: Friday, October 23, 9:11 PM
To: dhasenfuss@something.com

Dearest Danny,

I can too ask you to be nice to everybody. Why not? I'm not asking you to be friends with Kyle. Friendship can never be forced. But is it indeed so difficult to maintain civility and refrain from cruelty? I daresay John, too, thinks he's merely having a little joke and ensuring that he himself is not picked on by others. Neither justification seems to make his behavior any more bearable for you, and nor can you expect that your justifications can comfort Kyle. Please believe me that in the long run you'll earn much more respect by being respectful of others. Consider well the sort of person you want to be. Pardon the sententiousness – it's a privilege of old age, along with reduced rates at most museums and amusement parks.

Congratulations on another excellent vocabulary grade, as well as on your success in continuing to disarm your lab partner Rasheed. Our cunning scheme is undoubtedly working. Keep it up! I hope that your eye doesn't feel too sore any more, even if the discoloration remains. But don't consider it so awful to have a black eye - perhaps it makes you look plucky and devil-may-care.

As for my plans for the weekend, they consist of needlepoint needlepoint needlepoint again. I have just one more pillow cover to complete and I must be finished with that by Saturday evening. As long as Napoleon doesn't tangle up the works again, I should manage it. Saturday night is the big benefit auction for our new library, and the pillows are to be sold there to help raise money. At the moment I confess that needlepoint doesn't seem very exciting, but as you know, I always like the quiet life, so I suppose that's fine.

Yours in tedium, Grandma

From: dhasenfuss@something.com
Subject: **Re: Re: being nice to Kyle**
Date: Saturday, October 24, 7:06 PM
To: melbahasenfuss@another.com

Hi Grandma,

Okay, okay, fine, I'll do something nice for Kyle to make up for teasing him. (I just hope it doesn't turn out like trying to be nice to John did!) So I think what Kyle needs most is something to help him get himself together and be on time to class. Any ideas? To be honest I'm not sure if anything could help him – he really is such a loser, Grandma! A decent backpack to organize all his stuff? A jetpack to get him through the halls quicker? Probably he needs a combination of every kind of help he can get, and maybe a brain implant, too! (Just kidding. Don't worry, I won't say that to his face.)

My eye is still really sore if it gets pressed, but it isn't puffed up any more so at least I can see fine. Dad says I look more plug-ugly than plucky.

Eric should be here any second now. Dad's taking us out to a movie tonight! Bye!

     - Danny

Don't forget, if you have any ideas of what might help Kyle get to class on time for a change, let me know.

And here's the new vocab list: indomitable, oblivious, occasion, punctual, reluctant, scuttle

From: melbahasenfuss@another.com
Subject: **Re: Re: Re: being nice to Kyle**
Date: Saturday, October 24, 8:35 PM
To: dhasenfuss@something.com

Dearest Danny,

I'm pleased that you were so quick to understand my admonitions regarding Kyle, and so quick to repent of your behavior. As for ideas to help the boy, I can hardly give advice when I don't even know him, but I believe last month's issue of *Adventure Needlecraft* had instructions for a deluxe pack-everything rucksack designed to organize the intrepid adventurer for any contingency. I'll be happy to crochet one for the boy – out of Technofloss, of course, for durability – if you think he'd like it.

The pillows are finally finished, thank goodness, and in fifteen minutes I'm off to the library fundraiser auction gala thing. I'm dressed to the nines and I understand there's to be dancing, so I'm ready to paint the town!

Yours spiffily, Grandma

From: dhasenfuss@something.com
Subject: **Re: Re: Re: Re: being nice to Kyle**
Date: Sunday, October 25, 5:11 PM
To: melbahasenfuss@another.com

Hi Grandma,

The movie last night was great! The special effects were awesome, and there was this cool time machine wristwatch that was just what Kyle needs! I guess it would be pretty useful for anyone, for that matter. I wish I could invent that kind of stuff. I wonder if Rasheed is as good at gadgets as he is at chemistry? Oh, and the good guy got a black eye just like mine, except that it was already gone by the end of the movie. Mine's actually not too bad any more, either, at least compared with how it was.

Today was a little weird. At church Dad was talking with Connor's mom and invited Connor to come over to our house for lunch and the afternoon because his parents had to go to some urgent meeting with the lawyers or something. I sure didn't want him over, especially because Eric and I were planning to get together this afternoon! Parents can be so oblivious sometimes. I mean, it isn't as if it hasn't been obvious that Connor and I have hated each other since about second grade! So it was pretty embarrassing at first, but believe it or not it really wasn't that bad. It turns out Connor likes a lot of the same books I do, especially the science fiction ones, and we talked about that for a while, and he really liked the model spaceships I'd made. And then he said he used to make models, too, but John said they were stupid and he stopped! So I said he might as well start up again, because if John's not his friend anymore anyway, it doesn't matter what he thinks. And Connor smiled, and it made him not even look like a sewer rat any more. So we spent a while talking about how nice it would be if robots from space came and beat up John or something. And Dad gave us Swedish fish for snack.

Later in the afternoon Eric came over, and he didn't want Connor around any more than I did, but we played a

47

couple of games on the Wii and that was fun. Connor's actually really good at the baseball, and Eric is too, so they played each other a bunch. I'm not much good because I always hit too late, every time, so then Eric said that must be the way Kyle plays – always late. So we started making all these jokes about Kyle, and honestly Grandma, it was really funny. But then I remembered what you said and I suddenly got this great idea. I said, "You know what would be really funny? To make it a sort of project to see if we can fix him! I mean, like take him on as an improvement project and see if we can make him get to class on time and be, you know, like normal!"

Eric said, "Like a make-over? You've got to be kidding!" and started laughing his head off. And Connor said, "But no one does anything with Kyle. He's a total loser!" Well, I started to feel stupid for suggesting it, but I figured I couldn't back down now, so I said, "No, seriously. Wouldn't that be sort of a fun challenge? We could do it secretly, so no one would have to know it was us, and we could all try to think of different ways we might get him normalified. It would be like a sort of reality show, or even sort of a science experiment!"

Connor gave me a funny look and said, "You know what? This is why you're so much cooler than John. John would never think it was fun to help anybody. I say we do it." So that made me feel pretty good – Connor thought I was cooler than John! And after a little more grumbling Eric came around, too. So I told them about your idea for a backpack, which they thought was pretty weird but worth a try, and Eric came up with the idea of giving Kyle an anonymous phone call every morning at 7:20 to remind him he should be leaving the house now. Connor said he'd try to think of something. So how long do you think it'll be before you can get that backpack finished, Grandma?

    - Danny

Oh yeah, how was your fancy auction thing? And pet Napoleon for me!

From: melbahasenfuss@another.com
Subject: **Excitement at the Auction**
Date: Sunday, October 25, 9:52 PM
To: dhasenfuss@something.com

My dear Danny,

The benefit auction was indeed a success, although it didn't look very auspicious at the beginning. There were plenty of people of good-will there to support the library, and a number of prominent citizens, but unfortunately with this economy people just didn't seem to want to bid much money. The poor auctioneer was trying as hard as he could to whip people into a free-spending enthusiasm, but lot after lot was taken away after only modest bids. And then my set of needlepoint pillows came up. I didn't expect them to earn much for the library. After all, fifteen minutes earlier a gorgeous quilt had gone for only $275, which was a disgrace. But there were a few bids, and the price was up to $100 for the set. The auctioneer instructed his assistants to hold the pillows closer so those in the front row could "admire the exquisite detail and quality of these handcrafted heirloom treasures," and as the assistants paraded the pillows under the noses of the front row, he asked for $125... and to everyone's astonishment, a woman responded, suddenly throwing up her hands with an explosive exclamation! At the call for $150 she bid again, almost convulsively, while her husband next to her tried to shush her. And then I recognized her – it was the same woman whose life had been saved from the accidental gunshot at Carnegie's the other night, and I suddenly realized that she must be the wife of Martin Throgbottom, our town's wealthiest – and most notoriously stingy – citizen! At $175 Mrs Throgbottom threw up her hands and shouted out another exclamation, and then some of the others decided my pillows must be worth something after all. There was a flurry of bidding and the price quickly rose to $875 for the set. Then one by one the others began to drop out, but Mrs Throgbottom kept on bidding. Every time the assistant held out the pillow to her she gave an exclamation and threw up her hands again, even though her husband's increasingly frantic efforts to stop her seemed to be giving her great pain. Her eyes were red and streaming with tears, poor woman! $1100, $1125! There was only one more couple bidding against Mrs Throgbottom now, and Mr Throgbottom was actually trying to pin his wife's arms against her sides to prevent her from bidding, and she was rocking back and forth snuffling and shouting out. It was actually beginning to seem more than a little odd, and when the price reached $1500 and the auctioneer called out "Going once..." I heard Mr Throgbottom try to shout up to him.

"She's not bidding, you moron!" he screamed, "She's sneezing!" And then suddenly I realized what was happening. The pillow the assistants were holding under Mrs Throgbottom's nose was the one with a design of a handsome black cat. Exquisitely detailed work, it's true, but more importantly it was the pillow into which a fair quantity of Napoleon's fur had been embroidered by mistake. And Mrs Throgbottom, if you recall, was horribly allergic to cat fur. All this time, just as Mr Throgbottom said, she had not been bidding but sneezing! The auctioneer, however, appeared not to hear the objection, and proclaimed "SOLD! To the marvelously generous Throgbottoms for $1500!" with a triumphant bang of his hammer.

Mr Throgbottom jumped up to argue some more, but as he stood, before he could say a word, the crowd erupted with cheers. The library trustees rose to their feet with grateful tears in their eyes to give their generous benefactor a standing ovation, and everyone in the hall was stamping and whistling and cheering with excitement. And as Mr Throgbottom heard them, and turned around slowly to see the room applauding with delight for the unpopular miser's unexpected generosity, a

50

surprised smile slowly spread across his face. As you can imagine, with his reputation for stinginess, Mr Throgbottom had never had anyone much cheering for him before – and certainly not so enthusiastically.

Poor Mrs Throgbottom, who was only just now catching her breath and mopping her eyes and nose, looked around and whispered "What just happened?"

"My dear," the notorious miser replied with a beatific smile, "We have just turned over a new leaf. We are now officially Philanthropists."

"Are we?" Mrs Throgbottom said rather weakly, "How nice."

And after that everyone was so swept up with the spirit of giving that for the remaining lots the auctioneer could hardly raise the prices fast enough to keep up with the bidding. In the end the library brought in a very respectable $20,500, and the Throgbottoms bought not only my pillows, but several other items as well, and got credited with turning the entire fundraiser around. They could not, of course, take the black cat pillow for themselves, as Mrs Throgbottom couldn't so much as look at it without her nose starting to twitch again, so they donated that one to the library's reading room, and took the other three home for themselves. So that, I thought, was very gratifying to have been the inspiration (in however unconventional a manner) of such wonderful benefactors.

And now I'll give Napoleon your greetings and then get right to work on that rucksack for Kyle. It's a very complicated pattern and I'm really not sure how long it'll take, but I'll let you know once I have a better idea. I'm proud of you for turning a mean conversation about someone into an opportunity for kindness, and of course you're cooler than John. Everyone with a grain of sense knows that.

And speaking of good sense, I should assure you that your father is not as oblivious as you think. He's perfectly well aware that you and Connor haven't been friends, but he wanted to do what he could to help their family – for which I'm as proud of him as I am of you! You're both benefactors in your own ways. I advised your dad at the time that you and Connor would be able to get along fine. Will you allow me a modest "I told you so?"

Yours most affectionately, Grandma

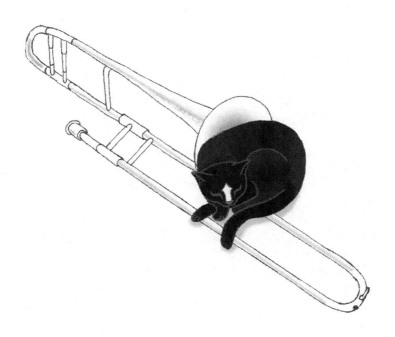

From: dhasenfuss@something.com
Subject: **Kyle progress**
Date: Monday, October 26, 5:47 PM
To: melbahasenfuss@another.com

Hey Grandma,

I can't believe you told Dad to invite Connor! You
don't know anything about these guys! I mean, it turns out
Connor's okay, but what if he wasn't? He's one of John's
gang for crying out loud! Or was, anyway. He ate lunch
with us again today and talks to us between classes as if
we were his friends now. At lunch Eric reported that when
he called Kyle's house this morning, some little kid
answered the phone and then shouted "Kyle, time to leave
for school now!" And then Eric heard Kyle in the
background say, "It is? Oh my god, it is!" and then the
phone was hung up. Pretty funny, huh. But you know
what? Kyle was just about on time to first period this
morning. Only about half a minute late, anyway, which is
better than usual. And at the end of class Connor helped
Kyle pick up his pencils and papers so he wasn't as late
as usual getting on his way to the next class, either. But
Connor was kind of embarrassed in case anyone saw him
helping Kyle, since after all he used to be in John's clique,
and he can't afford to have anyone think he's dropped
from that all the way down to Kyle! So he couldn't help as
much as we'd really want if we're going to transform Kyle
into the model of efficiency and punctuality we're aiming
for! :)

But I was so inspired by our success so far, and
Rasheed was being so decent in science that I asked him
if he was any good at inventing gadgets. He sort of
shrugged, which I took to be encouragement compared to
hitting me or calling me a loser, which he might just as
well have done. So I asked him if he could think of
anything that would help someone get to class on time. I
didn't mention Kyle, of course. Anyway, Rasheed went
"Hmmm... let me think about it." So I was hoping he might
come up with something. But now I don't think he will

53

after all. See, John and Marco stole my pencil case and played keep-away with it in the hall outside math, and they're both a lot taller than me so there was no way I could get it back. Then just before the bell rang John threw it as far down the hall as he could so I'd have to run after it and be late, only it happened to hit Rasheed, who was just running up. That made John and Marco laugh even more, but Rasheed was pretty mad and he whipped the pencil case straight at me. At least him throwing the pencil case at me meant I didn't have to run all the way down the hall for it, so we all got to class on time. (Except Kyle, of course.) But I bet Rasheed thinks it was my fault, and I don't think he'll want to invent any gadgets for me now – especially because by the end of school you could already see that my pencil case had given him a black eye!

Oh, and we presented our advertising projects in social studies, and everybody thought mine was a joke! For "celebrity endorsement" everyone else had like Hannah Montana and Tiger Woods, and I had Doris Dimond, the host of the TV show "The Knitters Knook." John said, "Is that your favorite show, Dan? What planet are you from where that's a *celebrity*?" But luckily Ms Rubel said, "Oh, my mother used to listen to Knitters Knook when it was a radio show. I had no idea it had crossed over after the invention of television!" So at least *someone* had heard of it. And for "play on emotion" I had the one with the picture of the baby in the pink fluffy cardigan that says "PERIL LURKS IN EVERY FIBER! Unless you're knitting with Allergex yarn, you could be exposing your loved ones to invisible dangers!" Eric started making jokes about The Sweater of Death, which cracked up the whole class. On the other hand, how much sillier is it really than the ad Sara brought in that tried to scare us into using Clorox disinfectant on every surface in the house all the time? I guess these ads are all pretty silly once you look at what they're really saying - but even so, your ads were definitely the craziest!

- Danny

From: melbahasenfuss@another.com
Subject: **Re: Kyle progress**
Date: Monday, October 26, 8:15 PM
To: dhasenfuss@something.com

Dear Danny,

What a great idea to recruit Rasheed for the Kyle Project. Does it occur to you that he might have known full well that John was to blame, and thrown the pencil case to you to be helpful, not vindictive? It's a possibility to consider, at any rate, and it's certainly worth talking to him again tomorrow. And while you're at it, can you think of anyone else who might have skills you could call on? Also, I do think that if you're serious about this mission you'll have to get over your embarrassment at being thought to associate with Kyle himself. It isn't as if paleontologists are concerned with being mistaken for dinosaurs, or geologists are embarrassed to be seen with rocks! When you take on a valuable job, you must take it on with pride.

I've been hard at work on the deluxe pack-everything adventurer's rucksack, and I think I just need a couple more days to complete it. I even brought it with me to work on during the subway ride when I went to meet a friend of mine for lunch downtown today. Actually, I'm lucky I didn't lose the whole thing and have to start all over again. I was walking the three blocks from the subway station to her house, and crocheting as I walked, as usual, when suddenly I felt a yank on my work. A large and very bold crow had grabbed the end and was trying to fly away with it! I said "Shoo!" and shook my end of the work, but the crow just held on tighter and pulled harder. I didn't want all my work unravelled, and I certainly wasn't going to give up and let it all go, so I started to run after the bird, trotting as fast as I could down the sidewalk, brandishing my crochet hook and scolding the fowl. I did get a few strange looks from passersby, I admit, but then, I'm used to being considered eccentric, so strange looks are nothing new. I don't know why the bird was so determined to steal my work, but crows are notorious for their love of shiny things, so I can only assume that this one was smitten by the idea of an entire nest made of a fiber with the unique iridescent sheen of Technofloss. At any rate, the enterprising crow pulled me down the street cawing at me just as indignantly as I scolded it, until I tripped over a Jack Russell terrier that was out walking with its owner. I'm sorry to say that the owner spoke quite rudely to me, but the dog was much more helpful. Intrigued by the sight of the half-a-rucksack that went flying past his snout, the dog leapt fully five feet into the air with a gleeful yap, and brought down my handiwork, and the startled crow with it. After a short, fierce altercation the crow relinquished its claim on the Technofloss and flew to the nearest tree to complain bitterly. The terrier proceeded to chew triumphantly on Kyle's half-a-rucksack. I asked the owner politely if he would remove it from his dog's teeth for me, and he had the nerve to suggest that I owed the creature something for having tripped over him! So I ignored the rude fellow and dealt directly with the management, who was much more pleasant. Indeed, I soon had him giving me big slobbery licks all over my chin, and happily exchanging the rucksack for a good petting.

I was afraid the treatment of the terrier and the crow between them might have ruined my work, but when I got to my friend's house and had a chance to examine it, I saw that I needn't have worried. Technofloss can withstand a good deal more than that!

Anyway, my dear, if you can see the silliness of advertisements, you're bound to be a much happier person, and of course a happy person is just what I'm hoping my grandson will be. So keep it up!

Fondly yours, Grandma

From: dhasenfuss@something.com
Subject: **crazy lunch lady**
Date: Tuesday, October 27, 7:23 PM
To: melbahasenfuss@another.com

Hi Grandma,

I think the lunch lady really is completely insane. When Connor came through the cafeteria line today I guess it was the first time she noticed him since he stuck up for me last week. She broke into a big, sappy smile and cried out, "Oh, Connor, what a brave, sensitive boy you are!" and flung out her arms – and the spatula flew out of her hand and smashed right through the ceiling light and there was a flash, and a bang, and some fizzling sparks, and all the lights in the serving area went out! "Oh dear! Sorry!" exclaimed Mrs Guglielmo with a cheerful giggle. But the principal, Mr Budge, heard the bang and thought it was a bomb or something, and evacuated the school, and in the stampede Drew stepped on a tater tot and skidded halfway across the cafeteria and brought down everyone in his path and flung his tray up in the air, and his apple hit Connor in the face and gave him a black eye, too. (Now there are five of us at school with black eyes, if you include Mr Budge. His is actually the worst of all. But mine is definitely fading. It's kind of yellowish now.) Then everyone had to wait out in the parking lot while the police bomb squad came and searched the cafeteria. And like five minutes after everyone else had cleared the building, Kyle came wandering out saying, "What's going on?" And the bomb squad came out and reported to Mr Budge what they'd found and we could see them handing him the spatula, and he let loose a string of cussing like we'd never heard. Even Marco was astonished, and he's got a vocabulary that can curdle milk! The bomb squad officer looked shocked and gasped, "Sir! The children!" And Mr Budge turned red as ketchup and muttered, "Oh, er, sorry. Everyone get back to class!"

57

Well, we went back to lunch, but no one could get food any more what with the destruction in the serving area, and there wasn't much time left by then anyway, so I shared my lunch with Eric and Connor. But poor Connor's never going to live this down. Now every time anyone sees him they all mimic Mrs Guglielmo's voice and squeal, "Oh, Connor, what a brave, sensitive boy you are!" And when John does it he flings out his arms like the lunch lady and throws plastic spoons at Connor, too. He must have grabbed a whole big box of them from the cafeteria during the chaos, and you might not think they'd hurt much, but they actually do. Some of them have like a sharp little nub of plastic on the end of the handle. There were plastic spoons thick on the floors in the halls by the end of school today. Last period we could hear Mr Budge crunching all the way up and down the hallway on plastic spoons, and muttering. I think he might be completely insane, too.

Anyway, with lunch interrupted we didn't get a chance to discuss our Kyle Project today. And I didn't talk to Rasheed, either. I chickened out when I saw how mad and mean he looks with his eye all purple and puffy. And I haven't come up with any more plans to deal with John and his gang, either. More advice, please, Grandma! Things are as bad as ever here!
　　　　- Danny

From: melbahasenfuss@another.com
Subject: **Re: crazy lunch lady**
Date: Tuesday, October 27, 9:05 PM
To: dhasenfuss@something.com

My dear Danny,

It sounds as if your lunch lady has a lot in common with Napoleon. Both, it seems, are hopeless romantics, for whom their rosy fantasies are more real than the mundane facts of their lives. At any rate, that's the only way I can explain Napoleon's foolish escapade today. I think he must have been fancying himself Emperor of the Wild again. When I opened the window this morning to put out a spider, Napoleon darted out again, no doubt intent on reclaiming his kingdom. Unfortunately for him, he'd no sooner started down the fire escape than that pack of feral dogs I mentioned caught sight or scent of him and set up a barking that could have knocked the pigeons off the telephone wires. Napoleon leapt six feet up and off the fire escape, with his fur bristled up like a porcupine, and came down on top of the lamp post near the back door. By the time I'd dashed downstairs and around to the back, there were six huge, mangy mutts standing guard around the lamp post, all barking and baying and taking turns to leap up and snap their teeth at poor Napoleon balanced precariously on top of the lamp in a frenzy of terror and fury.

Luckily for Napoleon the dogs couldn't reach him no matter how they jumped, and luckily for me, they were so intent on their prey that they paid no attention to me as I came up behind them, except that one of them turned and growled viciously at me before turning his attention back to the trapped cat. Nevertheless, at first I didn't know how on earth I could shoo them away and rescue Napoleon. It didn't look like Napoleon would be able to hold out long enough for the arrival of animal control, and I knew I'd have to deal with those dogs myself. I didn't

59

think it would be a very good idea to start beating them with a stick, and I had no steak on hand with which to distract them, but of course I do always have a crochet hook in my hair bun, so I drew my weapon and got to work. Within minutes I had crocheted those dog's tails together in a loop around them. The work was a little lumpier than my usual standards of quality, I admit, but in my defense, the dogs were constantly moving and the tails were constantly twitching, and I will say that my design was really rather attractive, almost like a pattern of flower petals encircling the vicious curs. Not that they appreciated my efforts. I was barely finishing the last stitches when they realized what I'd done and turned on me in a murderous rage.

At least, they tried to turn on me, but of course they couldn't. In their fury they began to chase around and around the lamp post, which was pretty much the only direction they could go. They got running so fast they were little more than a blur, and within ten minutes they exhausted themselves utterly, and sank down helplessly with their tongues lolling. They sort of reminded me of a Christmas tree skirt I tried to crochet once in my youth, although not, of course, in the same colors. At any rate, they were rendered helpless, and I called to Napoleon, who leapt off the lamp, right over the heads of the lying dogs, and into my arms. At least he had the grace to be grateful to be returned to his home. I hope he's learned his lesson about trying to escape.

As for the poor dogs, when the animal control men arrived they couldn't figure out how to get the creatures unhitched from the lamp post. In the end they had to bring a tow truck and lift the entire ring of dogs up over the top of the post (whimpering pathetically). I dare say they were able to work out the stitches once they got the dogs to the animal shelter.

You ask for more advice on dealing with the bullies at school, but it seems to me that you have all the strategies you need - unless you'd like to learn how to crochet. I'd

be happy to teach you at Thanksgiving. I think you'd find
it an extremely useful life skill – I know I have!
Yours fondly, Grandma

From: dhasenfuss@something.com
Subject: **last day of kickball**
Date: Wednesday, October 28, 7:42 PM
To: melbahasenfuss@another.com

Hey, Grandma,

Come on, you've got to give me some more help!
John still calls me mean names whenever he gets a
chance. He makes fun of my name and my black eye,
and my clothes, and my vocab quiz grades, and
everything, and all those guys poke me and stick out their
feet when I have to walk by and stuff. And now we've got
the plastic spoons flying around, too, whenever I'm near
Connor. And if you think learning to crochet would get me
teased less, you must be out of your mind! I'm tired of
getting picked on all the time! Please!!!!!

In PE today when we all have to wear shorts
everyone could see Marco's shin for the first time since
when he fell in the toilet last week. It's much worse than
my eye! It's all scraped up, and all around the scrape is a
horrible greenish-yellowish bruise. It must really hurt. But
Marco had more to worry about than the bruise hurting,
because of course everyone was asking him again what
happened and how he got such an awful scrape. He
repeated the weak excuse he'd given last week about
tripping while going up the stairs, and then he looked over
at me and gave a meaningful glare. I tried to give him a
sort of innocent and noble look as if to say, "Of course I
won't tell anyone, for I have given you my word, and I am
a man of honor!" but that's sort of a complicated message
to convey across a crowded gym with eyebrows alone, so
I don't know whether Marco actually got it. But at least
everyone's questions about his shin made it pretty
obvious that I hadn't told anyone yet, anyway.

We played kickball again, and I actually didn't do too
badly. John made his usual sneers, like saying, "You
want me to make your eyes match?" and stuff, but nothing
happened to give him any special excuse to pick on me,
and in fact he didn't kick or throw the ball at me at all. I

don't think he wanted another bump in the head any more than I wanted another smack in the eye! And the good news is, today was the last day of the kickball unit! I never have to play kickball again until next year! :D But the bad news is, Mr Viggles said we're starting the basketball unit next week, and I'm even worse at basketball than I am at kickball! And Hannah whispered to me, "I can't help you with that. I'm not that great at basketball, either." Man, I hate PE! But since she was being nice I asked her if she had any ideas for getting someone to class on time. I was too embarrassed to explain about the Kyle Project so I didn't mention any names, but Hannah said right away, "Is this for Kyle?" I sort of muttered something and she said, "I didn't know you were friends with Kyle." I denied it, and explained how we just thought it would be sort of fun to see if we could help such a hopeless case. She smiled at that and said she'd try to think of something, but then I noticed Marco glaring at me, and I figure he was mad at me for talking to her or something. I don't know why he doesn't just talk to her any time he wants. I mean, they're in the same clique, for goodness sake.

Did you really crochet up a bunch of wild dogs, Grandma? Dad says you must be exaggerating again, but I believe you. I bet you can tame any wild beast, can't you! You're like Supergrandma or something, even if you are totally insane! Anyway, I'm glad Napoleon's safe. Pet him for me!

    - Danny

From: melbahasenfuss@another.com
Subject: **Re: last day of kickball**
Date: Wednesday, October 28, 9:37 PM
To: dhasenfuss@something.com

My dearest Danny,

    I did not tame those feral dogs, of course. I merely incapacitated them. The good people at the animal shelter will have to tame those creatures, if any taming can be done. It's true that I have tamed some animals, though. Haven't I ever told you how I got Napoleon? He was quite wild when I first met him. It may not sound very impressive to tame a kitten, I admit, and a scraggly, scrawny little one at that, but he was a little black demon at first. This was about fifteen years ago now, well before you were born. One night he showed up in the parking lot, yowling half the night. He was tiny, but his yowls would have done a jaguar proud – or an elephant. Most of my neighbors threw things at him, and goodness knows I understood the temptation, but this only seemed to make him more determined. Someone called animal control, but Napoleon-to-be eluded them easily enough. (I've found that this town's animal control is usually effective in removing animals only when I've already captured the animals for them!) At any rate, by the time my entire building had been kept awake for a week by the dreadful caterwauling, I decided to take matters into my own hands. I bought some cat food and went out one night to confront the beast.

    Taming is, of course, about building trust, so I had to approach the wild kitten softly and gently. I spoke in a soothing voice, made no sudden moves, held out my hands slowly, and so on. You know how it works. Bit by bit I crept forward, murmuring sweet nothings, until I could leave my gift of cat food before him and then step back to sit quietly and wait. I also employed my own special strategy: crooning a soft song to soothe his savage breast. And finally, after about three nights, he was tame enough that I could pick him up and carry him to my apartment. The happy ending is that Napoleon is now the sweetest cat in the world, and he uses his disproportionately large vocal power primarily for purring. I have performed partial taming on the occasional tiger or police officer, but Napoleon's taming was certainly the most thorough. After all, it isn't as if I brought any of the police officers home to live with me.

Congratulations on surviving the kickball unit. Even if your basketball skills are worse, at least you know you won't be the only one who's no all-star. Stick together and you should be all right. I'm very sorry to hear that you feel things are as bad as ever at school. I confess I'd hoped that the Kyle Project would serve to alleviate some of your frustrations with your John troubles. At least you're recruiting more classmates to help with it, and I'm sure it'll be the more the merrier. I'm just about to put the finishing touches on the rucksack and I plan to take it to the post office this afternoon, so you should have it soon. Be sure to report to me how it's received! For my next project I need to get busy crocheting some monstrous spider webs for my needlecraft guild's Halloween party.

Affectionately yours, Grandma

P.S. If you change your mind about learning to crochet, just let me know. After all, don't forget that famous old saying, "The family that crochets together stays together."

From: dhasenfuss@something.com
Subject: **unsuccessful taming**
Date: Thursday, October 29, 7:34 PM
To: melbahasenfuss@another.com

Hi Grandma,

Well, I'm afraid your advice didn't work. Not even a little bit. See, in computer lab today my partner was Brandon, and he was being a total idiot jerk and driving me crazy. He kept pinching me and threatening to beat me up after school, while John and Madison laughed from the next computer station. Then I remembered what you said about Napoleon and police officers and all, and I thought it would be a brilliant idea to tame Brandon. Turns out I was wrong and it was a horrible idea, but of course I didn't know that until afterwards. But it wasn't my fault, Grandma, I did everything you said. I approached him softly and gently. When it was his turn at the computer I spoke in a non-threatening voice, made no sudden moves, and held out my hands so he could see I had no weapons. I offered him some Swedish fish, left them out on the table and stepped away from them, so as not to scare him. When it was time to change places at the computer I crept forward slowly and warned him what I was doing so he wouldn't be startled and turn defensive.

At first I thought it was working because he stopped pinching me and started staring at me with his mouth hanging open. But that didn't last very long before he said, "What the heck is wrong with you?" And then he said, "Hey John, are you watching Dan? He's either totally psycho, or he's possessed." John said, "So what's new about that? This is weenie Danielle we're talking about." Brandon laughed, but sort of nervously. Then I remembered your advice about the music soothing the savage bully, so I started humming something soothing – "Twinkle twinkle little star" was the first thing that occurred to me. Brandon began to back away from me. I smiled reassuringly and came forward slowly, my hands out, murmuring, "Don't worry, it's okay, Brandon. I won't hurt you." But he just backed up even faster - so fast he fell backwards over a chair and up against a table. That didn't stop him, he kept scuttling backwards like he was in a panic, going right under the table until he was up against the wall. By then the teacher asked what was going on and Brandon said from under the table, "Ms Mertle, Dan's acting all weird!"

Ms Mertle said, "Dan and Brandon, you can both settle down and get back to work." Well, Brandon came back over reluctantly, and we sat down at the computer together again, but he kept looking at me as if I was about to bite him. So I began humming again, very quietly. At that Brandon leapt up, grabbed his chair, and held it out between us. "Don't come any closer, man! I mean it!" he said.

I said again, "It's okay! Don't be afraid. I mean you no harm!" But Ms Mertle said, "Brandon and Dan, if I have to talk to you two again you'll both be coming after school." Brandon squealed, "No, Ms Mertle! Please! Don't make me stay after with him! He's freaky!" She asked me what I was doing to him and I said I wasn't doing anything, just trying to soothe him because he was obviously stressed out. So Brandon whimpered, "I'm stressed out because Dan's gone all wacked out. I think he wants to eat my brains or something!" John said "Why would anyone want to eat *your* brains, Brandon?" which was actually pretty funny, but I didn't laugh because I was still trying to tame him, and you said taming is all about earning trust. I just sang very softly and sweetly, "Up above the world so high, like a diamond in the sky..." and Brandon shrieked, dropped the chair, and vaulted over Ms Mertle's desk to crouch behind her. Needless to say, we got detention.

Not only did we have to come after school, but Ms Mertle got our advisor to come and counsel us. He sat us down across a table from each other and made us start by shaking hands. Then he asked us each to tell our side of the story. Brandon went first and said how I started acting all freaky and coming after him with my hands out like some sort of zombie or something, and humming at him like I was possessed, and how he'd seen a movie where the evil spirits possessed people and made them act just like that, and then they'd grab people's faces and sort of latch on and suck their souls out and their minds, I think, and then those people would be possessed and turn into zombies, too. So then when it was my turn I explained that he'd been pinching me and I was just trying to tame him so he'd leave me alone, and I'd never seen that movie and I didn't know what he was talking about.

Mr Phipps-Hinkle, that's the advisor, tried to come up with some kind of agreement between us, but in the end he sort of sighed and made Brandon say he wouldn't pinch me any more, and he made me say I wouldn't suck out Brandon's soul or eat his brains. Then he said, "Well, I'll leave these two to you to make up their work then, Ms Mertle." But Brandon jumped up and said, "I'm not staying here with him!"

Mr Phipps-Hinkle sighed again. "Brandon," he said, "Dan has promised he won't eat your brains." Brandon said, "Well, of course he's going to say that with you around, isn't he! But when he starts humming again, it'll be too late for me! I'm getting out of here!" That made Mr Phipps-Hinkle go all stern and say, "Oh no you aren't! You misbehaved during class, and now you'll leave when Ms Mertle says you can leave, and not before."

I tried to be friendly. Really I did. I shrugged at Brandon and smiled. He yelped, and shouted, "I'm not staying! You can't make me stay! There's nothing you can do to me - you're an advisor! What can an advisor do?"

Mr Phipps-Hinkle rose to his full height, with his head just about brushing the ceiling, and frowned down at Brandon, who was cowering beneath his frown, and replied fiercely, "What can an advisor do, young man? Why, I can... I can GIVE YOU BAD ADVICE!" And he stalked out of the room and slammed the door behind him.

Ms Mertle let us do the project separately, at different computers at opposite ends of the room, and I finished pretty quickly and left as fast as I could, but not before Brandon's eye had started showing a bruise. He must have banged it on the edge of the table or something when he fell backwards over the chair.

But before I left Ms Mertle said very sternly, "Dan and Brandon, there's to be no more of this nonsense in my class. But if there is, you'll be sent to Mr Budge next time, understand?" So now I'm on warning, I never even did anything, and for all I know Brandon will freak out again next time he sees me and there'll be nothing I can do about it! And who knows what he's going to tell John and their gang about all this tomorrow. By second period tomorrow the whole school's probably going to think I'm some sort of psycho possessed zombie! Now what should I do?

      - Danny

From: melbahasenfuss@another.com
Subject: **Re: unsuccessful taming**
Date: Thursday, October 29, 10:10 PM
To: dhasenfuss@something.com

Dearest Danny,

Had I known you would try to tame Brandon I might have suggested other techniques. The taming of humans must be dealt with somewhat differently from the taming of wild beasts. Still, it was very good thinking on your part to come up with the idea. As for failure, although Brandon certainly remains untamed, you might find that you can still deal effectively with the boy. Remember, while music can soothe the savage breast, it can induce all sorts of other emotions, too. When you watch a scary movie, for example, how do you know the scary part is upon you? Why, the music, of course! Think about it.

While we're on the subject of scary music, my poor trombone had a bit of an accident today. Napoleon's not as young and sprightly as he used to be, and nor has he ever been the most graceful of cats. At any rate, for whatever reason, this morning when Napoleon tried to jump up to his happy place on my trombone, he didn't quite make it. His paws reached the edge of the case, which must have been left a little too precariously on the edge of the shelf. He scrabbled to haul himself up, pulled over the case and the trombone with it, fell back to the floor, and brought everything crashing down on his own head. What a yowl he let loose! But the trombone's bell had landed on top of him, and his yowl just reverberated around his own ears. Meanwhile, the trombone had caught the lamp cord on the way down, and the lamp teetered for a moment on the edge of my desk and then came down on top of the case with a terrific shattering crash, making Napoleon yowl again. When I extricated the silly beast from the rubble, he streaked straight into my bedroom and didn't emerge for two hours. I, meanwhile, was left to clean up the mess. The desk lamp will need a new bulb and shade again, but these things happen, and luckily the trombone seems to be undamaged. I played vigorous New Orleans jazz for an hour or two just to make sure. I wonder whether the trombone will still be Napoleon's happy place now, or whether he finds his affection for it has cooled.

I expect you have your weekly vocabulary quiz again tomorrow. If so, good luck!

Yours fondly, Grandma

From: dhasenfuss@something.com
Subject: **vocab quiz**
Date: Friday, October 30, 8:00 PM
To: melbahasenfuss@another.com

Hi, Grandma,

    I'm not quite sure what you're saying about scary music, but I do know that it's scary how quickly John got to work on me this morning. The first time he saw me he said, "Oh look, it's weenie Danielle, the psycho possessed zombie nerd!" Brandon didn't laugh - he smiled nervously and made sure he wasn't near me - but all the others laughed. Rasheed said, "Wouldn't that be a great movie!" and Marco was like, "Yeah, just in time for Halloween!" and they all laughed at me some more.

    But then at the end of lunch Austin came by my table, and instead of saying something mean, he whispered, "Hey, Dan, you mind quizzing me on the vocab words?" Well, I think he must have studied more than usual, because he actually wasn't as bad as a couple weeks ago, but it's still amazing how hard he has to work to get the simplest words through his thick head! So I quizzed him through all the words about five times quickly, and then we went to English. I got 100% again, but I'll tell you something, Grandma, I had been spelling "occasion" wrong before I quizzed Austin, so it's really just as well he had me quiz him because it taught me that word, too! And when Ms Tulip handed back the quizzes Austin caught my eye and gave me a quick thumbs-up – and so did Ms Tulip! I don't know what he got, but it must have been better than he usually does. I bet Ms Tulip must have told Austin to ask me to quiz him. Oh, and he also said that last Friday at the end of lunch he was about to ask me to quiz him, but just then John and some of the other kids came by and he chickened out. So he hadn't been planning to smack me on the head with his lunch tray after all!

    But if you think this means Austin's our friend now, you're going to be disappointed. See, we went to science next, and we were doing a lab where we were mixing stuff in a flask with a big rubber stopper in it, and I don't know what Austin and his lab partner did, but their mixture started bubbling and sort of sizzling, and Austin pointed their flask right at me, and the stopper popped off like a cannon and came flying straight at me! I ducked and it hit Marco, and he started swearing fit to shatter all the flasks in the room, but everybody else was laughing like crazy, except Ms Diaz, who sent Marco to the nurse to get an ice pack for his eye and some soap for his mouth, she said. (I don't think they really do that, though.) But I bet Austin did it on purpose to hit me, so you can tell kindness isn't helping him any!

Anyway, no more John, no more Austin, and no more any of that gang until next week, so that's always good!
- Danny

From: melbahasenfuss@another.com
Subject: **Re: vocab quiz**
Date: Friday, October 30, 10:02 PM
To: dhasenfuss@something.com

My dear Danny,

    Congratulations on another 100%. Soon you'll be able to spell your way out of any situation. I recall as if it were yesterday the time Jeffrey Butchart threatened to beat up your Uncle Charlie. Charlie was only 7 or 8, and he panicked and ran into the woods instead of heading for home, and your dad went after him. Your dad had to leave a trail that I could follow to find them, but he also had to be sure that Jeffrey Butchart and his gang would *not* be able to follow the trail. Luckily he had a brilliant idea: he marked letters on the trees that led through the woods to Charlie's hiding place, but he also left letters marked on a lot of other trees heading in a lot of other directions, too. Jeffrey Butchart couldn't figure out which letters led the right way, and not only did he not find Charlie and your dad, but he got himself so badly lost in the woods that the police had to send in a search team. But I took one look at the letter-marked tree trunks on the edge of the woods and knew at once what to do. I started at the tree marked with an F, and from there looked for one with an L. Next I needed to find an O, then a C, then another C... As you can imagine there was no pattern here that Jeffrey Butchart could discover, but your dad and I shared a secret. We both knew a very special amazing word, and simply by following the marked trees in the order that spelled that word, I soon found Charlie and your dad safely hidden. The word, in case you'd like to learn it too, is floccinaucinihilipilification, and I bet if you ask your dad he'll still be able to spell it. As you know, "The family that spells together gels together!"

    I'm very glad to hear that you don't have two black eyes now, although I'm sure Marco didn't need a black eye in addition to his bruised shin. However, I respectfully submit that Austin's mishap with his flask stopper was exactly that: an accident. Don't be so quick to assume that you're the victim, and do continue to help him with his vocabulary. Some day it may be very handy to have him on your side.

Will you be doing anything for Halloween this year?

Yours fondly, Grandma

From: dhasenfuss@something.com
Subject: **Happy Halloween!**
Date: Saturday, October 31, 3:17 PM
To: melbahasenfuss@another.com

Hey, Grandma,

I asked Dad if your story was true, and he said you weren't exaggerating at all. And you were right – he could still spell your special word! But I tried to look it up in the dictionary and the nearest thing it had was "floccillation." Is yours really a real word? What does it mean?

Guess what - your backpack arrived today! It looks awesome! But it sort of reminds me of the thneed from "The Lorax," remember that? I hope Kyle can figure out how to use all those different pockets and compartments and stuff. It certainly is unusual.

We're not going to dress up or anything tonight. Eric says it isn't cool to trick-or-treat when you're in middle school, and Dad says I should stay home and give out the candy to the little kids, but Eric's going to come over for dinner and sleep over, so that should be fun. Did you say you're going to some sort of crochet Halloween party today? What do a bunch of crocheters do for Halloween, anyway?

  - Danny

New vocab list: apoplectic, bombardment, implement, incessant, frantic, solicitous

From: melbahasenfuss@another.com
Subject: **Re: Happy Halloween**
Date: Saturday, October 31, 11:51 PM
To: dhasenfuss@something.com

Dearest Danny,

Floccinaucinihilipilification is indeed a real word, although it's not one very many people use. If you couldn't find it you must have a "college" dictionary, which leaves out a lot of the words they think most people don't need. But everyone needs floccinaucinihilipilification! It means treating something as if it's worthless.

My needlecraft guild, The Loose Ends, includes not only crocheters, but also knitters, embroiderers, tatters, quilters, lace-makers, and more. This year we put on a "haunted house" Halloween party to raise money for the pediatric unit of the hospital. I was in charge of decorating and running one room of the haunted house, and I did a spider theme. I dressed as a huge spider, and I made the room into a sort of maze with only one possible way through the tangle of crocheted webs. It was great fun, and no one was permanently lost in the maze. There was a babysitter who disappeared around 6:30, but at the end of the night when I took down all the webs and rolled the thread back up into balls, I discovered her in a corner, all tangled up just like a huge fly. She said she yelled, but we just took the screaming for haunted house sound effects.

Anyway, I just got home and I'm ready to fall straight into bed as soon as I remove my excess arms, so that's all for now.

Wearily yours, Grandma

From: dhasenfuss@something.com
Subject: **crazy Halloween!**
Date: Sunday, November 1, 5:48 PM
To: melbahasenfuss@another.com

Hi, Grandma,
     Yesterday turned out to be a pretty strange
Halloween after all! Eric and I were just about to go to
bed, around 11:30, when we heard a noise outside. Eric
pretended to be all scary and said, "The zombies are
coming!" But I said, "I think it's even worse than that!
Listen!" And we heard John's voice! We went into the
bathroom with the light off and opened the window a crack
and peeked out. Drew was saying, "Shouldn't we wait
until the others get here?" John said, "They're late. Who
cares about them, anyway." Brandon said, "But they've
got the toilet paper," and John said, "But we've got the
eggs."
     I looked at Eric and whispered, "Uh oh. How can we
stop them?" Eric said, "Should we get your dad?" But I
was mad and I wanted to deal with them myself. I didn't
want John having yet another excuse to call me a little
baby tattle-tale! I said, "Maybe we can scare them away."
And then it hit me! What you were saying about the scary
music! And I put my mouth up to the window and sang
"Twinkle twinkle little star" sort of slowly and softly.
     "What was that?" squeaked Brandon, but John said
there wasn't anything. So after a minute I began to sing
again, a little louder, and Brandon said, "Seriously, dude!
Can't you hear that?"
     "What's your problem? Scared?" said John, and
Drew laughed. I whispered to Eric, "You keep singing,
and try to be creepy!"
     Eric said, "How can Twinkle Twinkle Little Star be
creepy?" but I said, "Just do it!" so he put his mouth to the
window and sang. We could hear Brandon whimper "Oh
my god, I don't like this! And it's Halloween!" Drew said,
"Quit it, Brandon. You're wigging me out." Then I ran
downstairs and snuck out the back door and crept around

the side of the house. When I got there they were arguing. John was saying, "There's no such thing as zombies, you big baby," and Brandon was saying, "How do you *know*? You guys didn't see the way Dan smiled when I called him one!" and Drew was saying, "Come on, Brandon, it isn't funny any more!"

Then I heard this faint "how I wonder what you are" that sort of floated down so you couldn't really tell where it was coming from. Also, Eric's really not that great a singer and it was sort of off-key, which actually did make it kind of creepy. Brandon said, "Oh my god, I think they're getting closer!"

John said, "It's probably just some baby's musical teddy bear or something, stupid," but I didn't think he sounded quite so confident. Drew said nervously, "I don't think Dan has a baby brother or sister."

"Dan *is* a baby," snapped John, "He probably sleeps with his musical teddy bear."

That's when I started singing, too. Brandon jumped about a foot in the air and yelped, "Oh my god, oh my god, oh my god! They're coming!" and I could see the light glinting off John and Drew's eyes as they looked around wildly in all directions. I stepped out of the shadows into the light from the streetlamp and held out my hands and said softly, "Don't worry, Brandon. It doesn't hurt," and I smiled. Brandon just let out a shriek and ran away as fast as he could go.

I turned to Drew and John, who were huddled together staring around sort of wildly. I shrugged and smiled, and took a step toward them. Eric started in on "Twinkle twinkle little star" from the bathroom window again, and Drew muttered, "Come on, man. Let's get out of here." John nodded and said, "Yeah. Uh, we'd better make sure Brandon doesn't get lost." "Right," said Drew, and they both turned and ran away after Brandon!!!

When I got back upstairs, Eric was still in the dark bathroom peering out the window. He whispered, "Check this out!" and I went over and looked. A car had just pulled up in front of my house, and Marco got out and walked up to the cartons of eggs sitting on the sidewalk, and looked around. (Eric asked, "Should we hum again? That was hilarious!" But I shook my head. There's no way we could scare all those guys, especially without Brandon to start freaking them out.)

We heard Marco say, "They were obviously here, but if they got tired of waiting why didn't they do the eggs before they left?" Rasheed's voice from the car said, "Oh well. This is stupid. Let's go back to your house." But just then another car drove up and stopped beside them and the window rolled down, and Hannah stuck her head out and said, "What are you guys doing here? Did you fight with John and those guys or something?"

Rasheed said "No. Why?" Hannah answered, "I'm on my way home from Madison's house, and we just passed Brandon running like crazy, and John and Drew about a block behind him, and they all looked scared to death. My mom pulled over so I could ask if they were okay, and Brandon didn't even answer, but John slowed down and said they were fine, but he still looked pretty scared."

Marco shrugged and said, "He said we should meet him here at this address, but we couldn't get my brother to drive us until he'd finished something, so we were a little late and they were already gone. No idea what could have scared them." He looked around as if he expected to see something scary standing there waving hello.

Hannah said, "What were you planning to do here, anyway?" Marco grinned and held up the stack of egg cartons he'd picked up, but Hannah said, "You were going to egg Dan's house? That is so pathetic. Seriously, I can't believe you guys are really that immature." And she rolled up the window and the car drove away. That wiped the grin off Marco's face, and he blushed so hard I could see it even in the dark across the yard. Austin's voice from inside the car said, "Come on, let's go." And Marco got back in the car and they drove away, too.

So that was our Halloween adventure, and you were sure right about the scary music, Grandma. I'd never have believed Twinkle Twinkle Little Star could have such a dramatic effect!

No news today, though, thank goodness! Except that I saw Connor at church and he said his mom's going to have to sell their house and buy a smaller one as part of the divorce. I told him Dad and I had to do the same thing, and having a small house isn't a bad deal – it means there's less space to lose your homework in. That made him laugh a little, but of course he's pretty stressed out. I'm really glad I didn't tease him about it back when I first heard.

      - Danny

From: melbahasenfuss@another.com
Subject: **Re: crazy Halloween!**
Date: Sunday, November 1, 9:24 PM
To: dhasenfuss@something.com

My dear Danny,

I'm glad to hear that you're helping Connor's situation instead of making it worse. That's the Hasenfuss spirit! It's hard to sustain being nice to people who are down – they generally aren't much fun – so if you can hang by Connor while times are tough for him, he'll probably only get better as his life settles down.

As for your Halloween adventure, good thing you figured out the power of music at such an opportune moment. And I suspect that Brandon will now be at your mercy any time he hears that tune – but you must be careful not to overdo it or the effect will wear off quickly.

As for me, I've had an interesting offer and I need to make a decision about what to do. Auntie Jane's Adventure Needlecraft Supplies, the makers of Hook-strong Technofloss, have asked me to be a product tester! This would involve a two week trek into deepest Tanzania for the purpose of testing Technofloss and other Auntie Jane's products in the wild. It's certainly a tempting offer as you know how I love my needlecrafts, and I'd be given all the supplies I could use, in addition to being among the first people to try out their latest technological developments. On the other hand, it would undoubtedly be an adventure, and you know how I always like the quiet life. Besides, what would Napoleon do without me? What do you think I should do?

Indecisively yours, Grandma

From: dhasenfuss@something.com
Subject: **Kyle Project**
Date: Monday, November 2, 7:25 PM
To: melbahasenfuss@another.com

Hi, Grandma,

Well, today was the day to implement the Kyle Project! Rasheed cornered me before social studies and I didn't know whether he was going to beat me up or what. But it turned out he wanted to give me the gadget he invented! I hadn't thought he was going to make anything after his black eye and all, but it turned out he'd been working on it pretty hard the whole time. He took the ringer vibrator thing out of an old cell phone and attached it into a digital watch, and he modified it so it could be set to start vibrating at one minute before the beginning of each class. Pretty cool, huh! And then before lunch Hannah pulled me aside, too, and gave me a pair of old roller skates that you can fasten to the bottom of your shoes. She said, "I thought they might help Kyle get to class faster." So during lunch Eric, Connor and I wrapped up the three gifts, and wrote a note to go with them. We wrote:

Dear Kyle, On behalf of the entire grade we'd like to see you stop being late to classes all the time. We've come up with 4 ways we thought we could help. One is the telephone call each morning to help you get to school on time. Second is this special backpack that should help you organize and carry everything you need, so you'll never drop your books or lose your homework or arrive at class without a pen. Third is the watch. It's already been set to vibrate at one minute before the start of every class. If you aren't to class by the time it starts vibrating, you might need number four – roller skates, to help you zoom through the halls faster. We hope you enjoy these gifts and find them helpful. Good luck!

Sincerely, Anonymous Benefactors

(We had a hard time deciding how to sign the note. The obvious thing would have been "anonymous friends," but none of us really wanted to say we were his friends. Eric wanted to sign it "The Kyle Project," but Connor thought he would get confused. Eric said, "So what if he's confused? He's always confused." But Connor said the whole point of the Project was to help him get less confused. Connor just wanted to sign it "anonymous," but I thought that wasn't friendly enough, and while we aren't really his friends, we don't really want to be unfriendly, either. So we finally decided on "anonymous benefactors." You gave me the idea from your fundraiser auction thing.)

So anyway, we left lunch a little early and left our package at Kyle's locker, and then hung around to watch. When he saw it he looked all around, but we all pretended to be busy at our own lockers, or tying shoes, or reading the bulletin board, or something. So then he read the note and opened up the bag and looked at everything with this funny look on his face like he was completely baffled and didn't know whether to be pleased or suspicious. But after a minute he started loading his things into the backpack, and then suddenly there was this loud buzzing noise that made everyone jump, and the watch, which was sitting on the bottom of his locker, started vibrating so hard it was sort of dancing across the locker floor. So then we knew it was time for us to get to class, too, and we left him there. Of course he was late to English, but at least he had everything with him! (And you'll be pleased to know that he wasn't sneezing, so either there wasn't too much Napoleon fur mixed in with the rucksack, or Kyle isn't allergic to cats.)

Last period Mr Zangway wasn't there when the bell rang. Kyle wasn't either, but a second later he went shooting by the classroom door flailing his arms and yelling "Whoa!" and then we all heard a crash. About half the kids got up and ran to the door to look out and someone said, "Kyle, what the heck are you doing?" Then he came rolling into the room rubbing his butt and saying, "Am I late?"

When John saw him, he said, "Oh my god, is this the disco era? Roller skates, digital watch, and a macrame backpack or something? Halloween was last weekend, Kyle, you freak!" But Hannah said, "I think your backpack looks pretty cool, Kyle. Madison, don't you think that's an awesome backpack?" Madison looked torn between being nice to Kyle and agreeing with Hannah, but finally she said, "Well, it would be an awesome backpack for a girl!" John said, "Where'd you get it, Kyle? From your grandma?" I couldn't help laughing at that, but Kyle just sort of sputtered and looked confused and said he didn't know. John said, "He doesn't know? I guess he doesn't know where his brain is, either." Brandon gave a sort of flinch and whispered, "Oh my god, I bet Dan sucked out his mind!" But John said, "Don't be stupid, Brandon. Kyle never had any mind to suck out, and it sounds like you don't, either." Brandon sat bolt upright and yelped, "Do you mean that? Do you think he's already possessed me? %*@#* you, Dan! You evil zombie! I can't believe you did this to me!" And just then Ms Mertle walked in.

She looked at Brandon, white in the face and shaking his fists at me, and said, "Class, Mr Zangway asked me to come and tell you to get started on the exercises on page 48 in your book. He'll be here shortly. But Brandon and Dan, I told you if there was any more trouble in class you'd be seeing Mr Budge, so let's go."

She marched us down to Mr Budge's office and sat us down in front of his desk, and said how we keep misbehaving, and then she left and Mr Budge looked sternly at us. At least, he tried, but it did look sort of funny with his black eye. In fact, all three of us had black eyes. Not that I thought it was too funny right there in the middle of being in trouble in the principal's office! Mr Budge said, "Well, boys, do you have anything to say for yourselves?" Right away I started to say, "It's not my fault, Mr Budge! I'm not doing anything and Brandon just keeps freaking out whenever he sees me!" but at the same time Brandon started in with "It's not my fault, Mr Budge! I'm not doing anything and Dan keeps trying to suck out my soul!" Mr Budge raised one eyebrow. I sighed. "Honestly, Mr Budge, I'm not a possessed zombie and I don't even want Brandon's soul."

Brandon exploded, "But he *looks* at me! And John said he thought my mind was already gone, and if it is then Dan must have sucked it out to possess me like those zombies always do, and I want my brain back!" Mr Budge tried to say, "I really don't think John meant that your mind was actually sucked out..." but Brandon just hollered, "Make him give me back my brain!"

Mr Budge said, "I think a little fresh air might help to clear our minds – which I'm sure we all still have," and he got up and opened the window. I could hear some voices from the sidewalk outside, and then, quite clearly, someone started to sing "Twinkle twinkle little star!"

Brandon jumped up, screamed, "They're coming from all directions!" seized Mr Budge's apple paperweight from his desk, and hurled it out the window at the zombie. There was a scream from outside, and Mr Budge let loose a terrible string of curses, until the secretary called out from the front office, "Mr Budge! The children!"

"Oh, right, sorry," he muttered automatically, but when he pulled his head back in the window he said, "They ran away. But what the #*@% were you thinking, Brandon?"

Brandon didn't answer. Mr Budge sat back down at his desk and took a deep breath as if he were counting to ten like Mr Phipps-Hinkle always tells us to do. Finally he said very calmly, "Brandon, there are no zombies, and you just threw my paperweight out the window at one of your fellow students. You are behaving irrationally and if this escalates I'll have no choice but to suspend you. In the meantime, I'm going to call your mother and tell her no more scary movies for you! Now, GET THE @$*#%* OUT OF HERE!"

So I, for one, got out of there. I didn't get any warnings and Mr Budge didn't call Dad, so at least everyone realizes that it's Brandon having issues and not me, thank goodness.

Anyway, now all we can do is wait and see whether Kyle can manage to use the stuff we gave him and get himself together. Rasheed wanted to take bets, but I honestly have no idea whether it'll work or not. Cross your fingers for us, Grandma!

About Tanzania, are you kidding? Of course you should go! (Unless it would make you miss Thanksgiving with us.) But this might be your only chance to see if Technofloss really can snare a charging rhino! And who knows what other awesome things you might get to try! I'm sure you can find someone to check on Napoleon while you're away. You've left him home before, like that time a couple years ago when you went to China to look for xenosaurs. Napoleon can handle it. And no one really believes you like the quiet life, anyway!

    - Danny

From: melbahasenfuss@another.com
Subject: **Re: Kyle Project**
Date: Monday, November 2, 9:47 PM
To: dhasenfuss@something.com

Dearest Danny,

I don't know what you're talking about saying I don't like the quiet life. Of course I do – it's never *my* fault I have so many adventures! The xenosaurs are a case in point. *I* never asked to go to China. It was a friend of mine who's a biologist at the university who asked me to join the expedition just because she needed someone who could kayak, sky-dive, translate the Guilin dialect, and identify and tag the reptiles. But you make a good point – this will probably be my only opportunity to explore the full range of capabilities of Auntie Jane's titanium all-in-one adventure survival crochet hook that was reviewed in *Adventure Needlecraft* a few months ago. Its solar-powered UV water purifier looks pretty nifty, and I'm particularly tempted at the prospect of using its cable-dart function. Plus, with its GPS tracking I can't get lost. Auntie Jane's makes lots of other interesting products, too. I might even get to try out the power-generating knitting needle set which is still under development. The rumor is that at 78 spm (stitches per minute) you can run an induction stove. The possibilities are intriguing!

I'm glad the principal seems to understand that you're doing nothing wrong. I'd hate to see my only grandson suspended under suspicion of felonious zombie activities!

As for Project Kyle, it sounds like you did an excellent job. Please be sure to report on its success.

Yours with crossed fingers and toes, Grandma

From: dhasenfuss@something.com
Subject: **Re: Re: Kyle Project**
Date: Tuesday, November 3, 6:56 PM
To: melbahasenfuss@another.com

Hi, Grandma,

When I got to school this morning, Austin had an awful black eye! Everyone was asking him what happened, and at first he said Mr Budge did it! He explained that he was leaving school with John and Madison yesterday and he asked them why Brandon was acting so weird. And John was explaining about how Brandon freaks out every time I sing Twinkle Twinkle Little Star, and when John sang the line, they heard a yell and Mr Budge's paperweight flew out the window and hit Austin in the face. Then Mr Budge came to the window and they all ran away. So I said it wasn't Mr Budge who threw it but Brandon, because he thought he heard zombies outside the window, and John and Madison about laughed their heads off, but Austin was pretty mad, as you can imagine. He's lucky he didn't get his skull cracked or something!

But the big news of the day is that the Kyle Project is a huge success! Eric called Kyle in the morning and he made it to school on time. He had all his materials in the deluxe adventure rucksack, and whenever he needed anything, he just reached right in and found it without any trouble. I wasn't sure that anyone else was particularly noticing, but Eric and Connor and I were giving each other thumbs-up every time Ms Quam said "Get out a pen" or whatever and Kyle did! At the end of class Kyle took a while to get all his stuff stowed properly and we were kind of hanging back worrying whether he was taking too long. But Rasheed whispered on his way past us, "You've gotta let him make it on his own," so we went ahead to art. And sure enough, Kyle skated up just before the bell! Actually, he had to stop himself by reaching out and clutching the doorway on his way past, so he obviously still doesn't have full control of the skates yet, but he made it!

89

Unfortunately art class wasn't so great. We're supposed to be doing self-portraits and John was sitting near enough to me to make nasty comments the whole time, like, "That's not very realistic, Fussy-fuss. It makes you look almost look normal. I think you need a few more zits." And he spattered red paint on my picture! And then he said, "And what about your clothes? I think they should look a little shabbier." And he smudged across my picture. And then he gave my portrait a black eye! Drew and Madison were laughing and making suggestions about how to make my picture look worse and how ugly I am and all. I was pretty upset about the picture because actually I thought I was doing pretty well, but I couldn't tell on John and have them think I was sucking up to the teacher again, and I just had to try to fix it as best I could. They tried to make fun of Kyle, too, and suggested he make his portrait include the roller skates and backpack and funny watch and a disco ball. But instead of getting upset about their teasing, Kyle said, "Hey thanks, that's a great idea!" and starting trying to draw the backpack!

So anyway, even if John was as much of a jerk as ever, the Kyle Project made it a good day! Kyle was on time to every single class all day, and when he skated into the math room last period, Mr Zangway said, "Wow, Kyle! The bell hasn't rung yet!" and Hannah started clapping. And the really funny thing was that just about the whole class spontaneously joined in cheering and clapping, and Kyle looked really surprised and pleased (and sort of confused, too, because after all, he's still Kyle). Mr Zangway looked like he might be about to yell at us for the commotion, so Connor explained that Kyle wasn't late to anything all day. Mr Zangway said, "That's certainly worth celebrating. Keep it up, Kyle!" Pretty cool, huh!

I'm dreading basketball tomorrow, though.

So, are you going to go to Tanzania? When do you leave?

     - Danny

From: melbahasenfuss@another.com
Subject: **Re: Re: Re: Kyle Project**
Date: Tuesday, November 3, 9:53 PM
To: dhasenfuss@something.com

My dearest Danny,

Congratulations on the preliminary success of the Kyle Project. But remember, one day isn't enough. This will have to be a long-term improvement for him. Keep me posted.

Yes, I've decided to take up Auntie Jane's's offer to test their new products. I leave early on Friday, so I have two days to make all my preparations. I'm crocheting myself a new multi-pocketed cardigan out of Technofloss to withstand the rigors of deepest darkest Africa. (It's bullet-resistant, too, but I certainly hope we won't be testing that!) I'm not working too feverishly, though, because of course I'll have a very long airplane flight during which to work on it before I arrive.

I've asked Mrs Szczepanski down the hall to look after Napoleon for me while I'm gone. She'll spoil him dreadfully, just like she does her three chinchillas and her hamster. She and Napoleon will both be quite happy, as long as she doesn't try to dress him up as his namesake like she did while I was in Patagonia last year.

Good luck with the basketball tomorrow! Maybe it won't be as awful as you think. After all, you run around, you bounce the ball, you throw the ball at a hoop. How bad can it be?

Optimistically yours, Grandma

From: dhasenfuss@something.com
Subject: **crazy basketball!**
Date: Wednesday, November 4, 7:39 PM
To: melbahasenfuss@another.com

Hi, Grandma,

Basketball was even worse than I thought! Although I guess we didn't really actually play any basketball. See, Kyle arrived (on time) on his roller skates, but before he could take them off, John came up behind him with a nasty smirk and gave him a big push. Kyle went shooting across the gym floor shouting HELP and wailing and waving his arms around franticly trying to keep his balance. Mr Viggles yelled, "Grab the rope and stop yourself!" so as Kyle went zooming past the climbing rope hanging down from the ceiling, he grabbed onto it. But he was going so fast that instead of stopping he swung right up into the air at the end of the rope. He screamed HELP again, and panicked and let go, and fell down into the basketball hoop, and wedged there butt-first.

Mr Viggles told him to push himself out, but Kyle wiggled and flailed and couldn't get himself free. "Okay, stay right there," said Mr Viggles, which seemed like sort of pointless advice, "I'm going to get the custodian to bring a ladder and we'll get you down." To the rest of us he said, "Everyone sit down, and there'd better not be any trouble while I'm gone!" which also seemed like pointless advice, though for the opposite reason.

Everyone sat down, but of course as soon as the gym doors closed behind the teacher, John said, "I bet that's the first time you've ever made a basket, isn't it, Kyle!" Then he said, "Come on, let's knock him down!" And he went to the big bin of basketballs and started pulling them out and throwing them at Kyle. John's a good enough shot that he was hitting Kyle more often than not, and all Kyle could do about it was put his arms over his head so he wouldn't get smashed in the face. Of course Brandon and Drew joined in, retrieving the balls as they came down and throwing them at Kyle again. And nobody said anything to stop it! Everybody else in class was either sniggering or looking like they were afraid to say anything.

I felt bad for Kyle, because how embarrassing is that to have your butt sticking through a basketball hoop ten feet in the air while people use it for target practice! And of course it was our fault he'd had the roller skates in the first place, so finally I figured John couldn't pick on me any more than he already does, and I said, "Quit it, John. Leave him alone." John just laughed at me and said, "You gonna make me, weenie Danielle?"

I said, "You'll be in trouble when Mr Viggles gets back."

"Only if some itty bitty baby loser tattles. But I'm sure not even the most pathetic loser in this class would want to risk what I'd do to a tattle-tale." He looked around at his gang and grinned, "Right?"

I looked around at his gang, too. Brandon and Drew were nodding and laughing, Marco and Austin were scowling, Rasheed was cracking his knuckles and looking like a Doberman, and Madison and all the other kids in class were looking like they'd just found a fabulous train-wreck reality show on TV. But Connor stood up with his face all red and said, "Quit it, John! Why do you always have to be mean all the time?"

John sneered and squealed, "Oh, Connor, what a brave, sensitive boy you are! How sweet of Convict Connor to feew sowwy for his itty bitty fwiend Kyle." And he threw the next ball at Connor's head, and then went back to trying to hit Kyle as hard as he could.

So I thought, if we couldn't make John leave Kyle alone, maybe we should try to get Kyle down ourselves. Eric and Connor agreed to help me with my plan, and I started climbing up the rope. Of all the things we do in PE, climbing the rope isn't too bad. I'm actually pretty good at that, so I went up pretty quickly before John and the other guys really noticed what I was doing, and Eric and Connor took the end of the rope and pulled it over toward the basketball hoop so that I was pulled closer and closer to Kyle. That's when Drew said, "Oh my god, look, weenie Danielle just wants to be near Kyle! Danielle and Kyle sitting in a tree..."

"Sitting in a basketball hoop," corrected John with a snigger. "Looks like he wants me to throw balls at him, too." And he did. I was reaching out from the rope to the basketball hoop when the balls started hitting me, and they really kind of hurt! Basketballs are a lot harder and heavier than kickball balls! I clutched onto the top of the backboard with both hands and tried to work my way to where I could reach Kyle. Then John whipped another ball at Connor, and I think it hit his funny bone. He let go of the rope, and Eric dropped the rope, too, and it swung away, and there I was, dangling by my hands from the backboard! Finally I managed to get one foot up, and pull a leg over so I could sit on top holding onto the bars that attach it to the ceiling, but now I was stuck up there, too! Drew kept singing "Danielle and Kyle K-I-S-S-I-N-G," and John was saying everything he could think of about how stupid we looked, and all three of them kept throwing basketballs at us, and John was right, because I know Kyle did look like a complete idiot, and I'm sure I did too! Then John said, "Come on, everyone! Let's get out the BASEBALLS and really have some fun!" Drew and Brandon ran to the supply closet to get the bin of baseballs, but when they came back Hannah said, "Okay, that's enough, John. Leave them alone!"

John said, "Oh, which one of these losers is your boyfriend, Hannah?" and Marco got all red again. But Hannah said, "Don't be stupid, John. Just because you wouldn't know what it's like to have real friends doesn't mean the rest of us can't stick up for ours."

Madison squealed, "Oh my god, Hannah! You just called them your friends!" And Hannah's like, "Uh, yeah!" And Madison said, "No way! How can you be friends with those nerds? They're the school's biggest losers!"

And you'll never believe what Hannah said, Grandma! She grinned and said, "Well maybe I'd rather be a loser like Dan than a cool kid like you!" And she grabbed the end of the rope and started to pull it over toward me again. Connor and Eric were just staring at her with their mouths gaping, but Marco was glaring at me again. And I had this moment of inspiration that you should be proud of, Grandma, and I caught his eye and gave him this look as if to say, "This is your chance to impress her! Side with Hannah now and she'll think you're a hero!" That's sort of a complicated message to convey across a crowded gym with eyebrows alone, so I didn't know whether Marco would get it, but after a second staring at me he winked with his one good eye and went over and grabbed the rope (with his hands just touching Hannah's!!!) "I'm with you," he said. "I'm not %#*@ going to leave Dan up there!" Hannah smiled and Marco turned redder than a Valentine heart. All the other girls in class started giggling, but John just looked meaner than ever. He took one of the baseballs and wound up to throw. But he didn't throw it, because when he tried, Rasheed grabbed his arm and knocked the baseball right out of his grip and said, "I think we're all a little tired of you now, John." And suddenly Austin jumped up and said, "Yeah! Who needs you, anyway!" The whole class gasped.

John said, "What the *#&*@ have you people been smoking?" but Rasheed and the others just turned away and ignored him. Rasheed climbed up the rope, and Hannah and Marco pulled it over toward the basketball net, and after a lot of straining, Rasheed and I between the two of us finally managed to pull Kyle out of the hoop. We helped him get himself turned around and grab onto the rope. Then Rasheed helped him climb down - which wasn't easy in roller skates! - while Austin and Eric stood underneath to catch him if he dropped. But he didn't, although he did manage to kick Hannah in the face. When he got his feet onto the ground he skated over to the wall and sank down against it with a relieved groan, while most of the kids cheered, and Marco examined Hannah's black eye solicitously.

I started climbing over the backboard so I could dangle from the hoop by my hands and drop down. I guess that's when John realized his prey was getting away. He looked around at everyone and said, "Well, come on Brandon and Drew. Don't tell me _you'_d rather be losers, too! Let's get him!" and they went to the crank on the wall and started raising the backboard up toward the ceiling! I grabbed onto the hoop but it was getting farther and farther from the ground so that I didn't dare drop down after all. I had to hook my knee over the hoop and hang onto the top of the backboard so I wouldn't slide down, and I couldn't cover my head or protect myself when they started whipping baseballs again. I tried to dodge as best I could, and a baseball thunked into the backboard right behind where my head had been! At least being up near the ceiling on top of the backboard meant they couldn't hit me so easily, but then Drew said, "Maybe we could break the backboard like they do in the NBA. Then he'd come down all right."

Connor said urgently, "We've got to get Dan down."

"The rope!" yelled Eric, "Someone throw him the rope!" So Marco took the rope again and tried to toss the end up to me, while John, Brandon and Drew kept trying to pelt me with baseballs. Every time I reached out trying to grab the rope as it went flying by I thought I was going to fall down on my head! John and Marco were both swearing, and the girls were all screaming, and another ball whizzed by, just missing my shoulder. Finally on about the fifth try, I managed to snag the rope. I got my feet untangled from the net, sort of half turned myself around, and let go of the edge of the backboard. Instantly I started to slide down, and as fast as I could I got both hands on a knot of the rope, pushed off with my feet, and went flying through the air, sweeping down in a huge arc like Tarzan! When I neared the ground I was going way too fast to let go, and I went shooting back up nearly to the ceiling.

On my way back down again I saw John, Drew and Brandon all taking aim to nail me as I reached the lowest point again. But before they could throw, Eric suddenly started humming, "Twinkle, twinkle, little star..." and Brandon yelped and dropped his ball and ran to the opposite side of the gym to cower in the corner. That distracted them as I whooshed by. Then Drew hesitated, and Hannah saw a basketball by her feet, and kicked it at him. It hit him in the back of the head and he screeched, "Ow!" and dropped the baseball to rub his head as I swooshed by again.

"Not very nice, is it," Hannah said, "You should have thought of that before doing it to someone else." But now I was at the top of the arc again, and John wound up, his eyes narrowed as he took aim... I closed my eyes, stuck out my feet in front of me, and braced myself. John screamed, there was a jolt in my feet, and I almost stopped swinging, but started spinning wildly. I opened my eyes and saw John flat on his back with his hands over his eye. I'd crashed right into him!!!

"Get off the rope!" hissed Austin, and I dropped off and managed to scuttle to my place along the wall just an instant before the door opened and Mr Viggles and the custodian came in, carrying a long ladder. John couldn't have been hurt *too* badly, because right away he sat up and tried to look innocent.

Mr Viggles looked up at the basketball hoop, which someone must have cranked back into place while I was Tarzanning through the air on the rope. He looked down, he looked around, he saw Kyle. He said, "Oh! You managed to get down by yourself, Kyle! Great work. You deserve extra credit in PE for that. But what are all these balls doing out? I told everyone to sit down and stay out of trouble!"

As fast as he could John spoke up in his best kissing-up voice, "It was Dan, Mr Viggles!"

Mr Viggles turned on me all ready to yell at me, but before I could even say a word, Eric, Connor, Kyle, Hannah, Austin, Rasheed, and Marco all yelled out at once, "NO IT WASN'T!" Not one of them would side with John! (And when Madison saw that it was John who was going to get in trouble, and he didn't seem to be such a cool kid any more after all, even she gave him a scornful look and scooted closer to Hannah again.)

Mr Viggles looked sternly at John, but he still didn't get a chance to yell at anyone, because just then the door opened and a couple of eighth graders came in. When Mr Viggles asked them what they wanted, they were like,

"Well, um, we have PE now!" Then Mr Viggles looked at his watch and said, "Uh oh! Class was over four minutes ago! You'd better hurry to your next class!"

Just at that moment we all heard a sort of faint buzzing sound. Instantly Kyle sprang to his feet, grabbed his rucksack, kicked off with the roller skates, and shot out of the gym, shouting, "My alarm! My alarm! We're going to be late!"

The rest of us followed as fast as we could, not even changing out of our gym clothes, but by the time we'd gathered our books and gotten to social studies, we were all several minutes late. Only Kyle was sitting at his desk, cool, calm, and collected, with his binder open to the right page in front of him, and his pen in his hand.

So, PE was a disaster, as usual, and basketball is off to a terrible start. On the other hand, maybe things around here won't be so bad any more after all. What do you think, Grandma?

    - Danny

From: melbahasenfuss@another.com
Subject: **Re: crazy basketball!**
Date: Wednesday, November 4, 9:26 PM
To: dhasenfuss@something.com

My dearest Danny,

I congratulate you on a successful adventure in PE. I can't help but suspect that it was hardly a representative sample of a day in the basketball unit, so you may find that basketball isn't as bad as you fear. On the other hand, maybe nothing can compare with the excitement of swinging through the air like Tarzan and finding that people actually respect you.

As for me, I'm getting ready to do my own Tarzan impersonation in the wilds of Tanzania. And just think – Tarzan had only vines to work with, but I'll have Technofloss!

In all seriousness, I'm proud of you, my dear, and I hope some of these new relationships will become friendships and the rest will at least remain courteous.

Yours fondly, Grandma

From: dhasenfuss@something.com
Subject: **a normal day???**
Date: Thursday, November 5, 7:12 PM
To: melbahasenfuss@another.com

Hi, Grandma,

I can't believe it - nothing awful happened today at all!
John has a black eye now from when I swung into him on
the rope in PE (and of course Hannah got a black eye
from Kyle's roller skate). That makes ten of us. Or at
least, it would, except that mine is finally really gone now,
and so is Kyle's, and even Mr Budge's ladled eye looks
almost back to normal.

Of course while everyone was working on group
projects in social studies John started in on me as usual,
but the amazing thing was, no one would laugh or join in
at all! Brandon whimpered, "Please just don't make him
mad, John!" But Rasheed said, "Dan's cool, John. Give
him a break." John said, "Dan Fussy-fuss? Cool? Are
we still talking about the same loser who thinks spelling is
fun, and kicks like a girl, and dives headfirst off the
bleachers, and kisses up to Kyle, and wears clothes like
that? Come on, Rasheed, when you said 'cool,' you must
have meant 'most pathetic loser in Edgar Middle School.'"

But you know what, Grandma? All that stuff he said
didn't even matter to me any more, because I knew
kicking like a girl had made me better in PE, and being
nice to Kyle had made me better friends with Connor and
Rasheed and Hannah, and the clothes... well, I know my
clothes aren't exactly the coolest, but they're okay, and
I'm not asking Dad to buy me the sort of stuff John wears,
so there's no point in worrying about that either. So I just
looked at John and said, "John, you can keep up with the
floccinaucinihilipilification all you want, but it doesn't mean
a thing to me." And then everyone laughed and Austin
said, "Flocci-whatever doesn't mean a thing to me, either,
Dan. Thank god that's not one of Ms Tulip's vocab words.
I bet you'd never manage to teach me that one!" And I
said I bet I could, and so at lunch the whole bunch of them

sat with us and I tried to teach your special word to everyone! Then we all tested each other on the vocab words for tomorrow's quiz. And when John and Drew and Brandon went by with their trays, Marco just gave them one hard look, and they didn't even try a thing!

Kyle was on time all day again, so I think we can definitely declare victory. On the other hand, we really didn't succeed in normalifying him. He's still definitely weird. But he's totally mastered the rucksack and always knows exactly where everything is. Marco and Hannah both think the rucksack is the coolest thing ever and they asked if you could teach them how to make backpacks for themselves when you're here for Thanksgiving! The thought of Marco crocheting totally cracks me up – but if he and Hannah learn, maybe you could teach me, too.

I hope you have a great time on your trip, and I'll see you at Thanksgiving!

    - Danny

From: melbahasenfuss@another.com
Subject: **Re: a normal day???**
Date: Thursday, November 5, 8:38 PM
To: dhasenfuss@something.com

My dearest Danny,

I'm so glad to hear that the bully problem has been neutralized at last. It sounds like you're finally ready to take my original advice on dealing with John: just ignore him. Congratulations!

Napoleon can tell I'm leaving and is doing his best to get underfoot while I try to work. He sends you a purr and looks forward to seeing you for Thanksgiving, too. But now I must finish up my packing.

I leave for Tanzania at 5:00am tomorrow, and I'm very excited, as you can imagine. While I'm gone, good luck on your vocabulary quizzes tomorrow and next week, and on all your endeavors in school. I'll see you on the 22nd, and I'll be delighted to teach you and any of your friends how to crochet. Who knows – maybe I'll have learned some new techniques or discovered some interesting new products to show you, too. After all, once you know how to crochet and how to spell, there'll be nothing in this life you can't accomplish! Or at least, it's a darn good start.

Yours affectionately, Grandma

More Books by Anne E.G. Nydam

Hey, Diddle Diddle! and Other Rhymes

Kate and Sam to the Rescue
Kate and Sam and the Chipmunks of Doom

Song Against Shadow
Sleeping Legends Lie
Return to Tchrkkusk
Vision Revealed
A Threatening of Dragons

Visit **www.nydamprints.com**
for more information!

Made in the USA
Middletown, DE
20 November 2017